Dark Reign of Destiny

Isla Thornton

Contents

1. Chapter 1 — 1
2. Chapter 2 — 7
3. Chapter 3 — 11
4. Chapter 4 — 15
5. Chapter 5 — 19
6. Chapter 6 — 24
7. Chapter 7 — 28
8. Chapter 8 — 32
9. Chapter 9 — 36
10. Chapter 10 — 40
11. Chapter 11 — 44
12. Chapter 12 — 49
13. Chapter 13 — 54
14. Chapter 14 — 58
15. Chapter 15 — 63
16. Chapter 16 — 68
17. Chapter 17 — 73
18. Chapter 18 — 77

19. Chapter 19   82

20. Chapter 20   89

21. Chapter 21   95

22. Chapter 22   100

23. Chapter 23   104

24. Chapter 24   108

25. Chapter 25   113

26. Chapter 26   118

27. Chapter 27   122

28. Chapter 28   131

29. Chapter 29   135

30. Epilogue   141

1

Chapter 1

I was walking home from my literature class when I accidentally got in the middle of an angry crowd. It was a bunch of people protesting something but I wasn't quite sure what they were protesting in the first place. I tried to push my way through the crowd when suddenly someone had shoved me into the middle of the road. If there hadn't been any cars on the road I would have been fine but unfortunately for me I was hit by an oncoming car. I wished for another chance as I closed my eyes in that world for the very last time.

I was suspended in nothingness for a while, I couldn't tell how long I was there and I didn't care since I was at peace. Then something came along and disturbed me. It was a woman with beautiful long snow white hair and a long flowing white dress. Her face was a blur to me but I could clearly hear her voice. "Apologies my child, that was not the way your life was meant to come to a close" She told me softly like a mother speaking to her young child "You were destined to find your soulmate in that world and fall in love and start a family together while you flourished in your career as a musician!".

I felt a sense of lost of what could have been, I felt a tinge of sadness for my soulmate in that world that now no longer had a soulmate. His original destiny was also ruined by my accidental death. "I'm afraid that we can not send you back to that world" She informed me solemnly. "However the other gods and I have agreed to honor your last wish and grant you another chance at life!" She told me on a happier note. "That's great but" I began but she cut me off. "Good luck my child, you'll need it!". Left on that ominous note I slowly started to drift downwards and slowly started to lose conciseness again.

When I awoke I had a pounding headache and I was sore all over. I tried sitting up but it was futile. I was far too weak at the moment to move on my own. I slowly moved my little hand to my forehead...wait a minute...my hand is small now...WHAT ON EARTH HAS HAPPENED!?!?. Despite being weak and in a lot of pain my panic managed to get me to roll onto my side and look around for the closest mirror. Luckily the side I had turned on had a mirror facing the bed directly.

A young girl with ghostly white skin and long wavy raven black hair with eery pale blueish green eyes stared back at me. That little girl had to be me. What happened to me? I tried to piece together what happened but my memories came to me in a confusing way. It was not just one person's memories it was both the memories of this little girl and my own. I remembered walking back from class with my noise foolishly in a book like always, I recalled playing outside at sunset and one of my maids was calling me to come in since it was getting dark. I remembered with an ice cold shiver down my spine being pushed into the way of a car, I recalled from the little girl's memories that she had tripped over a lone branch in the garden and had hit her head and had knocked herself out.

After a few minutes my strength began to return to me, I began trying to sit up on the huge luxurious bed I was on that was covered in bright pink sheets. It took me a few tries but I managed it. I then attempted to stand up and lean against the bed for support so I could look at my new body in the mirror fully.

I admit in my pervious life I was quite vain and I guess some old habits die hard. I was now short and petite, before I was tall and lanky. I looked to be around eight years old. I digged around in the girl who I reincarnated as memories to see if I could find exactly how old I was in this world. It seemed that my tenth birthday had just passed. In my pervious life I was eighteen years old and in college studying literature while starting out my career as a musician. I was in a band with a few of my friends, I was the lead singer and I played the piano.

My goodness what were they going to do without me now. We were meant to play a gig that night, it was meant to be the start of our music career. I felt like bawling my eyes out, I missed my friends, I missed my family and my pets. It seemed like the girl I now was didn't have it easy. She may have been nobility but her parents despised her and ignored her existence were ever possible, she had no real friends from the look of it and her fiancé also didn't like her since they had absolutely nothing in common. Wait hold on a minute...a fiancé? THIS GIRL WAS ONLY TEN YEARS OLD FOR PETE'S SAKE WHY DOES SHE HAVE A FIANCÉ!

It has been a day since I woke up in this knew world and I have uncovered something slightly terrifying. The girl I was now was a lot like the villainess in a romance novel I had loved to read in my previous life. Her name was Lady Raven Darksheild, guess what! THAT'S ALSO MY NAME NOW!.

The similarities don't stop there oh no the place she lived in was exactly how it was described in the novel and the people around her... yea also featured in the novel and matched their novel counterparts exactly except that all of them were younger. This had me come to the conclusion that I am now the villainess Lady Raven Darksheild but I was reincarnated before the plot of the novel takes place. I am starting off life in this world in her childhood which meant I had time to prepare and prevent the horrible death that awaits Lady Raven. Do you want to know how she dies in the novel? SHE GETS BEHEADED BY HER EX-FIANCÉ AFTER HE LEAVES HER FOR THE HEROINE.

Granted Lady Raven did try to murder Ashley, the name of the heroine, but she was angry and hurt that her fiancé who she loved with every fibre of her being cheated on her and had the audacity to publicly break off the engagement and within the same breath proclaim that he and Ashley were then engaged. Quite honestly I don't blame Lady Raven for how she reacted, Lord Timothy had destroyed her reputation and humiliated her in front of the entire nobility in the kingdom. Her life had basically been ruined right then and there since he didn't just stop at breaking off the engagement, no he began to slander Lady Raven. Lady Raven wasn't even the worse villainess in the novel.

Lady Tara and Lord Harvey did far worse things to the heroine, they had relentlessly bullied the heroine and had nearly killed her on multiple occasions. The worse thing Lady Raven ever did to Ashley was making a few snide remarks here and there or gossiping about the heroine within earshot. Lord Harvey was barely punished at all for what he had done to Ashley, the love of his life broke up with him but that was it. He didn't get thrown in jail or killed. No one even mentioned anything about him after his fiancé broke off their engagement.

Lady Tara who was the most terrible of all the villains in the story just got thrown in the dungeons for the rest of her life. It was unfair to how Lady Raven was treated compared to the other two villains. It was about time I started coming up with a plan. I had to avoid Lady Raven's original end at all costs. The only problem was I had to figure out exactly how to do it without drawing attention to myself.I could just tell that bad things would happen if I strayed away from the original plot of the novel too much.I came up with a plausible plan.

1. Do not get attached to Lord Timothy, you can be friendly to him but DO NOT UNDER ANY CIRCUMSTANCES FALL IN LOVE WITH HIM IT WILL END BADLY.

2.Be nice to the heroine Ashley! Yes she may be the other woman who your fiancé is cheating on you with but control your anger and jealously. You can do way better than men like that slimeball of a man that is Lord Timothy Bainne.

3.Make some actual friends, they could be a great help to save your reputation if Lord Timothy decides to start slandering you after he breaks off the engagement.

My plan seemed foolproof, it wasn't too complicated and it was vague enough that I wasn't being held back by too many constraints. Now that that matter had been dealt with it was time to put my plan into action but first I had obligations to attend too. I was only a day in to being a noble girl but I was already tired from all the things I had to do.

Who knew that being nobility with its strict rules and etiquette would leave you so tired and emotionally drained at the end of the day. Once again I missed my old life and the simplicity of it. I also missed my phone, there wasn't much for me to do here while being couped up in my room since my maids wouldn't let me out since they were worried for my health. Well at least someone in this world cared for me, even if only a little bit.

2

CHAPTER 2

The scent of cherry blossoms was in the air as I walked towards the conservatory of the grand mansion on the Estate of Duke Armin Rondish. This was where I was to meet Lady Tara. Lady Raven had already met Lady Tara a few times but this would be my first time meeting her.

If Raven's memories served me correct then they weren't close friends but where in the same friend group. I needed to first befriend Lady Tara and make her my best friend so I can tell her not to bother the heroine in the future so I don't get dragged into the mess she and Lord Harvey made with the heroine and the male leads. I know what you're thinking, "Lina why are you befriending her? Shouldn't you try to stay away from her!". While yes staying away from her would work for a bit but Lady Tara would still bully the heroine if I didn't become friends with her so it is better for me to befriend her and get her to trust me enough that she'll actually leave the heroine alone.

There was five other girls in the conservatory with us. I waited patiently for a gap in the conversation where I could talk to Lady Tara directly. Lady Tara was small and very skinny, she had long straight dark red hair and dark green eyes. She has a small button nose and had a light dusting of freckles on her face and arms. In the novel it said she had a signature colour which was red which she wore all the time and it was the colour that suited her the best. In the novel Lady Raven also had a signature which was pink but it did not suit her at all.

I decided to incorporate some of my style from my previous life into this life. In my old life I was a goth. I wore heavy makeup and dressed in dark clothing. My room also reflected my style and was dark but also had classical elements which you would see in vampire movies that revolved around a castle. My parents didn't really like my style but they were supportive none the less. Right now there was nothing I could do about my new room, it had to stay bright pink for now until an option to change it comes up.

My clothing on the other hand was an easy fix. Lady Raven had a few dark coloured dresses to choose from but there was also a lot and I mean a lot of pink clothing in her wardrobe. I chose a long dark grey dress with lace on the cuffs and hem of the dress for the tea party. Before I left the estate that morning I had looked at myself in the mirror and thought I looked good in it. It seemed Lady Raven looked good in dark colours, this would be good for me since I planned to slowly throw out the pink clothes and exchange it for greys and black clothing. Of course I'll keep a few just incase I need to wear a pink dress. That wouldn't be likely though.

The other four girls I recognised from the novel were Lady Raven's and Lady Tara's friends who they were seen chatting with a lot. One of them happened to be Lady Sophia. Sophia happened to be the daughter of a baron who made a lot of his money in the dessert trade. Sophia matched the description of the novel, she was a short plump girl with a very kind and adorable face. In the novel Sophia doesn't bully the heroine but she also does nothing to stop it because she was afraid of Lady Tara taking her wrath out on her instead. She had shoulder length brown curly hair and had the prettiest big brown eyes and dark skin.

I made a mental note then and there to befriend her as well. An opportunity to speak to Lady Tara reared it's head and I took advantage of the moment. "So ladies what do you think of the new dress boutique beside Madame Oscar's dress boutique?" Lady Tara asked as she took a dainty sip of her tea. "It is does not live up to expectations!" I told the girls while carefully choosing my words. In the novel I remembered a particular line where Lady Tara goes off on a rant about how Madame Oscar's boutique was the best place to get a gown made and then the heroine disagrees with her and saws that Mrs Mattison's was the best place to get a gown made.

To become Lady Tara's friend and get close with her I must agree with her opinions and chose my words carefully to avoid offending her. I needed to get her to trust me and be able to confide in me, that way I'll be able to help her like any good friend would and keep her from going down a bad path. "Quite right Lady Raven!" Lady Tara smiled while giving me an approving look. "Well said Lady Raven!" Lady Sophia commented sweetly. I gave her a smile in return. It seemed like befriending these girls wouldn't be a hard task but it would be a long journey to gain their complete trust.

The tea party was a success, the conversation continued to go in a way that benefited me and I dare say that the ladies present there now have a some what high opinion of Lady Raven, which is me. I heard no mention at all about Lord Harvey I guess I would meet him at some later date in the future. I was sitting in the carriage on the way home with my personal maid Sandra.

Sandra had her dark blond hair in a tight bun and she looked to be in her late twenties. "M'lady I've been asked to remind you to write to your fiancé" Sandra told me while looking for something in the basket she had brought with her. "His letter arrived two days ago and you haven't even opened it". I stared at Sandra for a moment and then I remembered that Lady Raven didn't just have to deal with six young ladies who she had to befriend at all costs, she was also engaged and that meant she had to write letters to her fiancé and occasionally visit him.

I considered for a moment whether to actually bother with the engagement. In the novel Lord Timothy didn't care at all for Lady Raven and only replied to her letters out of obligation and not because he wanted to and every time she visited him he would always act so cold towards her. "Must I Miss Sandra?" I asked with an innocent but sad tone. Sandra was absolutely shock by my words, normally Lady Raven wouldn't hesitate to write to her fiancé. "Why would you say such a thing? Of course you have to m'lady he's your fiancé!" Sandra scolded me.

"I just get the feeling that he doesn't like me very much!" I told Sandra while looking so very sad. Sandra gave me a look of pity, I should become an actress I was nailing faking my true feelings. "I'm sure he just needs to get to know you better young lady, I'm certain by the time you two are to be wed you'll get along like a house on fire!" Sandra reassured me but I could tell from the look in her eyes that she was uncertain about that prospect. I guess she also knew that Lord Timothy didn't like Lady Raven and was now slightly panicking what her and the other servants were to do now that Lady Raven was suspecting that her fiancé didn't like her like she liked him.

3

CHAPTER 3

When I got back to the Darksheild estate I had to remind myself that I had to act like I was in love with Lord Timothy even if I wasn't. I think I was going to give Sandra a panic attack if Lady Raven's personality change a bit too much in a too short space of time. Sandra had given me Lord Timothy's letter and had told me to write something to him before it was bedtime so the letter could be sent in the morning. I returned my room which looked like a pink fairy had barfed pink all over it.

The amount of pink in the room started to hurt my eyes, I would need to find a way to solve this problem but first I had a letter to read and then I had to write one myself. I walked quickly over to the desk beside the balcony and opened the letter with a envelope knife. Honestly who would give a ten year old a knife to open mail!!. I opened the letter and was disappointed but not surprised by what I found inside. The letter was quite short and lacked any emotion behind the words. How on earth did Lady Raven not realise her fiancé didn't like her, it is clear as day that he doesn't like her by how plain and boring this letter is.

Dear Lady Raven,In regards to your last letter I am fine and I thank you for asking. I am afraid I am not available to meet you for lunch this week but I can schedule it in for next week if some event gets cancelled I will write to let you know! Goodbye for now, Lord Timothy Bainne

I rolled my eyes while reading the letter, he didn't even ask how Raven was. I was outraged for the poor girl that I now was. I guess I should stop referring to Lady Raven and Myself as two separate people. I was her now and there was no changing that so I guess I had to fully become her while still staying true to myself. I considered how to reply to this letter which I took as a symbol of disrespect since he didn't even bother to ask after my health.

I picked up an ink pen and ink pot and a couple sheets of writing parchment. I would first draft the letter and then fix the wording here and there to make it seem more realistic to what a ten year old noble girl would write in this world. I had to keep reminding myself I was ten years old again and not eighteen. Oh this was so weird, mentally I was years ahead from my peers but I had to act like them, ugh I couldn't wait to grow up. After a couple hour of writing and rewriting a letter I finally finished it and was quite happy with the result.

Dear Lord Timothy, How are you doing at this time? I am writing to you in regards to a different matter than I usually write to you about. Over these past few days since I got your letter I have been reflecting on our engagement and I have come to the conclusion that we are not a good match. Therefore I would like to set up a meeting with you whenever you have a bit of spare time in the coming weeks.

I have been in doubt of your feelings towards me Lord Timothy and your latest letter has confirmed it to me. You did not ask after my well being in your letter and the overall tone of the letter made it seem like our engagement is a burden to you so I would like to fix that.

Whether it would be best for us to continue being engaged or for the engagement to end is up to you to decide! I believe I have made my feelings for you quite clear during our engagement and now it is time for you to truly decide what you want and whether or not you want to be in an unhappy marriage or a happy one. I would advise you to choose wisely Lord Timothy for I do not give second chances to people who reject me and my feelings! Kind regards,Lady Raven Darksheild.

I read over my letter again and decided it would be best to see how he would react to me trying to break off the engagement. If he does break off the engagement then it will be his choice and I will not get the blame for ending the engagement. This could give me a chance to get out of this relationship early before he turned even more resentful towards me for being trapped in an unhappy relationship. I sealed the letter with wax with my family's personal stamp and set it on the desk for Sandra to get it delivered.

I didn't have to wait long for a response. Just two days letter Sandra came into my room as I was sorting through the clothes in my wardrobe much to the dismay of my other maids. I had asked Sandra after I had written my letter a few days ago if I could go shopping for some new clothes. Sandra asked my parents for permission and they didn't care as long as I wasn't bothering them. My father handed Sandra some money for her to give me so I could buy things with. It was more money than I had ever held in my pervious life. I stopped purging the hideous pink dresses and took the letter gently from Sandra's hands and thanked her for bringing it to me.

Dear Lady Raven,I have read your letter and am angry that you doubt my feelings for you. I accept your request for a personal meeting and shall be expecting you at Bainne Manor on Wednesday morning before 10 o'clock!Regards,Lord Timothy Bainne.

I had to stop myself from laughing at the letter. I doubted whether Lord Timothy actually cared for Raven. He probably felt threatened that Raven would want the engagement to end so he's trying to cling onto her to prevent her from leaving him. It was really quite funny considering what he is going to do to their relationship in the future. After crumpling up the letter in my hands and throwing it in the bin much to the surprise and horror from my maids.

I looked to Sandra and asked as sweetly as I could "May we please go shopping now Miss Sandra I need to get a dress for when I visit Lord Timothy on Wednesday!". If Sandra was shocked by Lady Raven throwing out a letter from Lord Timothy which she usually locked in a safe and guarded it like a dragon guarding it's golden horde I couldn't wait to see how she would react to me picking out outfits in greys and blacks when Raven would have chosen only pink outfits. This life wasn't so bad after all!

4

CHAPTER 4

We were headed into local town and I couldn't contain my excitement. Finally I wouldn't have to see the colour pink in my room. Depending on the price of the dresses I might also but new sheets and maybe wallpaper if I had money to spare. Sandra brought me to Madame Oscar's boutique and I headed inside gladly.

The boutique smelled like vanilla perfume and wildflowers. A plump middle aged woman came out from behind the register with a long peice of measuring tape draped over her shoulders. "Greetings young customers how may I help you today?" She asked in a very professional voice. I smiled prettily at her. "Good Morning Madame Oscar" I greeted her politely "I am in need of a few new dresses so I hope that you can help me in that regard!" I told Madame Oscar like how any other noble woman would have asked if they came in for a new dress.

Madame Oscar smiled warmly at me, not just because I was smiling at her but because I had manners which couldn't be said for many children of nobility that go shopping with their servants without their parents in sight. "If you follow me young lady to the fitting room we shall them discuss exactly what you are looking for!"

Said Madame Oscar as she showed me the way to the fitting room in the back of the shop. Sandra followed me dutifully.

The fitting room was small and had three full length mirrors against the walls. There was one chair beside the door and Sandra sat down on it while she waited for me to be finished getting my clothes fitted. Madame Oscar didn't just sell custom clothing she also sold prepare clothing that she would then alter on request. "Now young lady what is it you are looking for in particular?" Madame Oscar asked me as she measured my arms. "I am looking for dresses in blacks and greys!" I told her confidently while holding myself as still as I possibly could.

"For any particular occasion?" Madame Oscar inquired as she measured my height. "Some for very day wear, some for more formal occasions and a few night clothes!" I informed her. She asked me about my budget and I told her the budget was two hundred Highmoorns(High Highmoorn is the currency in the country Highmoorshire which is the country Lady Raven currently resides in). This was two thirds of my budget as I wanted to save some money to redecorate my room. Madame Oscar showed me a few premade dresses that were simple but they would do nicely for everyday wear.

She had me fitted for a few formal dresses for me to wear when I would go visit friends. Raven had already debuted so I didn't have to worry about that. I also bought a few nightgown that I liked and I even bought a navy blue dress with the dress budget that was left over from the other dresses and I still had a hundred Highmoorn for room decorations. My formal dresses would be delivered to my family's estate in a few days time, just in time for my meeting with Lord Timothy. The premade clothes would be altered by my family's personal seamstress since I didn't want to wait very long to wear my new dresses. Sandra had the bags of dresses in her arms as we made our way through the crowed business streets on the search for stores selling the things I needed to get to truly make my bedroom my own.

I had bumped into Lady Sophia and her mother in the shop selling wallpaper. I chatted with Sophia for a few minutes and managed to sneak in a few compliments here and there which were gratefully received from Lady Sophia. Baroness Karen called for her daughter to rejoin her and Sophia and I said our goodbyes to each other as we got on with our day. I spent half an hour picking through the available wallpaper much to the dismay of my maid Sandra. "M'lady do you really need new wallpaper?" She asked me disgruntledly as she rearranged the bags on her arms.

"I do, my room looks to childish!" I stated firmly. I couldn't tell Sandra the true reason I was changing my room decor. I had to make it seem like some whim that many children have when they want to appear more grown up than they were. Sandra sighed but didn't say anymore on the topic. I happened to come across a wallpaper with black Ravens in it surrounded by a dark grey. It was perfect. I bought four rolls of that wallpaper, I hoped it would be enough.

I bought a few black bedsheets and curtains and even a dark grey rug. I had everything I needed to redecorate my bedroom. I was very excited on the carriage ride home. Oh if Raven's parents ever bothered to visit her room after it had been redecorated they would had been absolutely shocked by what they would see.

Anything that was bright in colour was thrown out and was replaced by dark colours. Instead of the bright pink wallpaper they had bought for their daughter when she was first born was gone and in its place was a dark grey wallpaper with ravens all over it. The pink bedsheets that had only been bought a few weeks previously had been mysteriously burned during the night. The bed was now covered in satin bedsheets and the very frilly and pink decorative pillows that Marquess Eric Darksheild had sent one of his butlers to buy for his wife Lady Elinor, who then gave the pillows to her daughter because she hated the pillows where now chucked into the very back of the wardrobe and would be repurposed at a later date.

Every thing in the room was now very gothic. Lady Raven's maids hoped she was just going through a phase and would go back to having her room very colourful before her parents found out. Unfortunately for them this change was permanent, just wait until they see I have gotten rid of very pink clothing item I own I thought savagely as I imagined their faces of shock and horror. Oh how I'll laugh in private once they leave. Hey I may be trying not die like the villainess Lady Raven but that didn't mean I couldn't be at least a little bit of a villainess for fun from time to time.

5

— · —

Chapter 5

Sandra woke me up at five in the morning on Wednesday for me to have time to get ready. I swear the amount of makeup they put on me was ludicrous for a ten year old girl to wear. My face was completely caked in makeup I had refused to have any pink makeup applied to my face.

My maids decided to leave my hair down that day, not because they thought the natural waves in my hair pretty but it was because we were running out of time. Sandra rushed me through the halls of Raven parents' Manor, who I haven't come across yet in my time here. When she got me outside the house I almost ran into someone. It was a tall man with long raven black hair and a sharp jaw line with equally sharp cheekbones just like Raven had or she will have once she grows up.

His skin was more tanned than Raven and he had rounded shoulders. Raven must have gotten her square shoulders from her mother then. He looked me up and down with a disapproving glare because this man was Marquess Eric Darksheild, Raven's father. "Good Morning Father" I greeted him with a small curtsie while avoiding meeting his eyes. He narrowed his eyes at me, he could tell that something wasn't right about me.

My heart started to falter as I thought about the possible things he could have noticed. "My goodness why are you dressed like you're going to a funeral?!" Marquess Eric exclaimed while glaring at Sandra for an explanation. Sandra struggled to come up with any other reason than "because the young lady wanted to".My father glared at me for an answer, "I like the colour black more than pink and I believe that the colour black suits my skin tone better than pink ever did!" I told the Marquess while staring at my feet to avoid looking into his furious eyes at that moment.

The Marquess seemed a bit lost for words at that moment, probably because he was trying to consider how much he should yell at me for dressing in dark colours against his and Raven's mother's instruction. After a minute of him taking a few deep breaths and clenching the bridge of his nose in annoyance he finally decided on how to reprimand me. "Go to your room!" He ordered swiftly while turning his back to me and walked away.

"But I have a meeting with someone!" I called after him in a panic. He turned around in disbelief "Who could you possibly be meeting that is so important you would defie your father's orders?" He interagated me while stomping over to Sandra and I. "My fiancé!" I told him plainly. "Well just send someone to say you won't be able to make it" He told me angrily. "I believe he wants to end the engagement!" I lied. Lord Timothy may or may not have loved Lady Raven during this period of their life but his letter made it seem like he wanted to fight for the survival of their relationship so I'll give him the benefit of the doubt for now.

I messed up by telling my father that Lord Timothy wanted to break off the engagement. Because it was now him, Sandra and I all sitting in the carriage on the way to the Bainne's Estate. He was coming because he was outraged for me, no he was coming because he felt offended that the son of an Earl would dare try to break off an engagement with a Marquess's daughter, especially when said son would be the one to inherit the title and land of the Marquess and Earl in time since women couldn't inherit property in this world. After I've saved myself from being beheaded I should think of starting a women's rights movement. I did try telling him he didn't have to come and that I could handle the situation myself but he didn't trust me. This was going to be one very uncomfortable carriage ride.

I was sitting in a pure white sitting room with my father sitting in an armchair by the fire with Earl Thomas Bainne, they would be acting as shaperones today. They didn't even bother pretend to read a book, they just stared at us, fully listening to me and Timothy's conversation. Timothy had short blonde hair and brown eyes and a square jaw. He was a bit taller than me at this stage. He had broad shoulders.

Timothy waited for me to speak, to explain myself. Well he would have to wait just a bit longer, I had to incorporate my lie as much as I could into the conversation so that I wouldn't get murdered by Raven's father for lying to him. I wouldn't be surprised if he did do something like that. "It is as clear as day that since the start of this engagement you have not been happy about it!" I stated calmly. Timothy tried to denie this. "No I've been happy about being engaged to you" He lied quickly.

To our fathers sitting in the corner they believed what he said more than me. "No you have not!" I accused angrily "you barely look at me and in the four years we have been engaged you have barely said more than two sentences to me at a time!". He tried to denie this but I interrupted him. "You barely know me, I know so many things about you but you barely know anything about me!" I said while holding back fake tears.

If I was going to make Marquess Eric believed what his daughter has been saying then I needed to show the appropriate amount of emotion in this situation without appearing too dramatic. "I do know things about you!" He lied once again. "O really?" I said unconvinced "then what's my favourite colour?" I asked him knowing he would fail either way, in the book Raven's favourite colour was pink which was evident from the colour she was associated with the most.

However if he said pink I was going to say black but I was curious to know if he actually knew her favourite colour in the first place. "Um..."He faltered as his mind created a blank space, he didn't know her favourite colour. "G-green!" He proclaimed, he was so proud of himself for giving an answer he thought was right. I shook my head sadly and let a single tear run down my cheek.

"That's your favourite colour" I sniffed sadly while taking the handkerchief I had in my sleeve and dabbing my face. Marquess Eric and Earl Thomas were horrified that Timothy didn't even know Raven's favourite colour and was foolish enough to mistake his favourite colour for her favourite colour. Timothy was embarrassed by his monetary lapse in judgment. Meanwhile I was displaying my newly found acting skills, I looked like I was absolutely distraught from my fiancé not even knowing surface level information about me.

The next few hours we were in the Bainne's Manor were the most uncomfortable hours I've experienced in this world yet and I've only been here a week! Marquess Eric and Earl Thomas discussed what they were going to do about the situation. Neither of them had been aware of how bad the situation had become. They knew that Timothy didn't like Raven very much but they hadn't noticed that he barely spoke to her and didn't even know the most simplest bits of information about her.

It seemed like my engagement to Timothy would go ahead, I was horrified to know that our fathers thought the best course of action for us was to force us to spend even more time together. Timothy was sulking in the corner after his father took him outside for a few minutes to scold him for his behaviour towards me for the last four years. My father didn't really know what to do with a crying daughter so he just patted me on the head and keep saying "there,there" over and over again. Honestly if I didn't have to keep up the distressed child act I would had punched him. Like sir your child is upset at least say something better than "there there".

I found out when I got home that Timothy and I had to see each other on Saturday every single week for at least an hour so we could get to know each other better. That seemed like a very good way to build resentment. It seemed like I would have to find another way to break off this engagement before the heroine comes into the picture but I had other more pressing matters to occupy myself with. I had private lessons to study for and I had a tea party to plan. I was a very busy lady indeed.

6

CHAPTER 6

I was now fourteen years old and next year I would be joining the magical academy where the male leads would meet the heroine. Of course they wouldn't meet her until we were all seventeen so I still had time to prepare for the worst. It seemed like Marquess Eric and Earl Thomas's idea to force Timothy and I to spend more time together was sort of working.

The first few weeks we barely said a word to one another, I actively ignored him. It was until one particular Saturday where we had to be in each others company for six hours when we finally started speaking to each other. It took quite a while but we were now on okay terms, we were friends even. On a happier note my mission on becoming friends with other ladies was going beautifully. I was best friends with Sophia and Tara and was on a first name basis without titles with them.

I also became close to the other girls in my friend group. Lydia, Michelle and Nina were their names and we meet up at each others houses regularly and attended lessons together at the private school we all attended before we would go off to the academy. I still hadn't seen Lord Harvey anywhere, he wasn't at any social function I went to and he wasn't in my classes so I wondered where he was. I did meet his fiancé Lady Helena, she was such a nice girl. I could see why she brought off her engagement with Lord Harvey in the future when she found out about the bullying. I also became friends with her as well and we write to each other regularly.

It was a Saturday morning and I was walking through my garden with Lord Timothy. We were discussing plants, Lord Timothy really liked plants and knew a lot about them. What he was saying about plants was rather interests so I listened avidly. We somehow got onto the topic of marriage. "Raven I've been meaning to ask you something" He told me quietly as we walked through the row of red roses. "Yes what is it?" I asked a bit timidly. I was nervous as to what he would ask. "You know how we are to be wed at the age of twenty" He began nervously. "Yes" I said softly as a hint to encourage him to continue.

"Why'd you think they picked that particular age?" He asked me curiously "I've heard from others that they getting married younger, eighteen years old for example!". I pondered this for a moment, I've never really given it much thought before. "If I had to guess I would say they picked twenty to make sure they picked the right partner for us!" I guessed nonchalantly. "That doesn't make much sense" Timothy told me. "It makes a little sense" I replied "It is only natural for them to want to make sure that if you assume the title of Marquess that you would be fit for the role". Timothy nodded and we continued our walk around the garden.

I was in the middle of my music lesson when my mother came barging in. "Raven go and get ready we have leave in a few minutes for the ball" My mother exclaimed as she rushed about the place with a trail of servants following behind her. I swear she was getting more and more be bizarre by the day. I was more surprised by the mention of a ball, i wasnt aware that one was happening tonight.

I went to my room as I was told and rang the bell for Sandra to come. While waiting for Sandra I went to my closest to pick something to wear. I chose one of my black formal dresses with lace and ribbons in similar colours to the accessories I picked out. All my jewellery were silver, gold just made me look so washed out. After spending an hour getting ready I finally joined my parents in the carriage, well it was just my father since my mother was still getting ready. After waiting twenty more minutes for my mother to hurry up getting ready she finally dashed out the front door.

My father helped her into the carriage and she sat beside him while I sat opposite them. When apart they were some of the coldest individuals I have ever met when together by the god of darkness they made no secret of their love for one another. I believe I forgot to mention I recently chose to worship the god of darkness in this world, Oiche. Never of them knew about my conversion to darkness, both of them worshipped the goddess of leadership, Ceannaire, so they would expect me to worship her as well.

I just found that there was more benefit for me to worship Oiche than Ceannaire, no I didn't convert just because the god Oiche matched my gothic lifestyle. My parents also couldn't fully wrap their heads around the idea that their daughter preferred dark things to things of bright colours. They still think I'm just going through a phase and that I'll go back to bright colours soon. That is not very likely.

The carriage ride to the Grand Royal Palace was uncomfortable, but I had to get used to my parents being all lovey-dovey in front of me. They would not be changing how they show affection any time soon. I was happy that I could spend the entire ball with my friends since they all would be here. Of course Tara would be dragged away from us every now and again by her fiancé, the second Prince of Highmooreshire Prince Edward Stormbrood.

Prince Edward is another male love interest for the heroine. By my positive influence Tara was not quite like her novel counterpart. Most of her personality was still the same but she didn't seem as malicious as she was in the book, of course there no way of truly knowing if she has changed for the better until the heroine starts to steal Prince Edward away from her. When that happens I'll be there by my best friends side, comforting her like any good friend would. I did truly care for the girl.

I found Sophia in the corner by herself. Her parents still hadn't arranged a marriage for her but she didn't look bothered by it, she seemed happy without a care in the world. "Sophia!" I said happily as I approached her with my arms open wide to pull her into a hug. "Raven!" Sophia said as she matched my energy and returned my hug. "Why are you standing all by yourself?" I asked her concerned "where's Tara, Nina, Michelle or Lydia?". Sophia smiled at me and reassured me that they were alright they just got dragged away for one reason or another and would be back soon.

Sophia and I made our way towards the refreshment table and walked away with glasses of fruit juice in our hands. We didn't risk trying to take one of the glasses of wine, that would have caused a scandal we could do without. Sophia and I chatted about a full bunch of things while we waited for our friends to appear. Over the course of ten minutes Lydia, Michelle and Nina showed up and we caught a few glimpses of Tara being walked about the place with her arms linked with Prince Edward.

7

CHAPTER 7

Tara finally managed to escape from her fiancé's clutches and we, being the good friends that we were, were hiding Tara from view as best as we could. Quite honestly it was a little scary how good we were at hiding things when we were all working on it together. I could see how in the novel the male leads didn't know the extent of what the villains in the novel did until the heroine told them towards a few chapters before they kill off the first villainess, aka me. "So how has your evening been so far Tara?" I asked Tara with a bit of merriment to my voice.

We all knew how exhausting it was to have to be on show all the time and not let your guard down at all but we still liked to joked about it with each other. Tara smiled and joined in with my joking mood. "If I have to smile one more time I'm going to go on a murdering spree!" She laughed and we all laughed along knowing that she was joking of course. The Tara we knew wouldn't have considered killing someone, even for a second. Which couldn't be said for the book version of her. Out of the corner of my eye I saw Lady Helena headed our way with a young lord on her arm. I recognised the young lord's name by his appearance. A tall boy with long brown hair and silver eyes and a hooked nose.

This had to be the young version of Lord Harvey. "Enjoying the evening Lady Helena?" I inquired politely as they approached. Lady Helena smiled warmly and had her usual cheerfulness and friendly demeanour around her. "Quite so Lady Raven I thank you for asking" She replied in the correct manner. "I want to introduce you to my fiancé since I consider us such good friends!" She informed me. "I would be delighted to make his acquaintance!" I said while smiling at Lord Harvey. He gave me a stiff smile in return.

"Darling!" Lady Helena said while turning to Lord Harvey "This is Lady Raven Darksheild ". 'How do you do!" He said quickly, his words didn't require an answer since they were what were usually said when you were introduced to someone for the first time and didn't want to appear rude. "Lady Raven this is my fiancé Lord Harvey Shineblade". "I hope you are well!" I said in the same tone Lord Harvey used when greeting me. Lady Helena stayed and chatted with us a while. Lord Harvey had told Lady Helena that he had to go speak with a few people but would be back in a few minutes. That was about an hour ago. And there was no sign of him returning anytime soon and none of us cared.

Prince Edward came up to us three times in the last hour looking for Tara. We told him we hadn't seen her while Tara had hid behind Sophia. I had to suppress my laughter until he had walked away again. My own fiancé hadn't approached me at all and I was fine with that. It's not like we would get married anyway, once the heroine was in the picture he would leave me for her. I could only hope that our tiny bit of friendship with one another was enough for him to not slander me when he finally ends it. We walked around the ballroom for a while and stopped to chat with our peers every now and again. We had to stay out of sight of Prince Edward since he would have dragged Tara away from us the second he saw her. I swear that boy had separation anxiety when it came to his fiancé.

The night was finally coming to a close and though I had fun my feet were hurting and I just wanted to go to bed. I meet back up with my parents and we entered the carriage to go home. "I noticed you never joined in a dance with your Fiancé!" My mother began and I knew she was about to go off on a rant about how I needed to try harder to like my fiancé and what not. Then my father added to the conversation about how mother and him didn't like each other when they got engaged but learned to love each other by the end of it. I wanted to yell that it may have worked out for them but that's now what wad going to happen to Lord Timothy and I.

When I got ready for bed I didn't head to my bed immediately. Inside I went over to my little alter beside my desk by the balcony. There was three black candles on it with a badger skull in the middle with a complicated drawing within a circle underneath it. I quickly lit the candles and said a few prayers to Oiche. When I was finished I extinguish the flames and went to bed. However I didn't go to sleep just yet. I had finally met Lord Harvey. I now had to decide what I was going to do about him. Lord Harvey didn't like the heroine because he was quite a classis.

Meaning he looked down on anyone who was lower than him on the social hierarchy. I could befriend him since in the book he is friends with Lady Tara. His relationship with Lady Raven was never really talked about. They could have been friends or they might not have been. I decided to let nature take its natural course with this one. As long Harvey doesn't do anything too drastic then Tara and I shouldn't get involved just by being associated with him. I dreaded for the time for the heroine to appear to come. That would mean I would finally see if all my effort over the years would mean something or if it would all end in failure. With those unsettling thoughts I finally drifted off to sleep.

8

CHAPTER 8

Two weeks, just two weeks until the heroine Ashley is due to arrive at the academy with us. The new term had already started but she would be joining us a bit later. I hope I have done enough to prevent Lady Raven's original ending.

I sat in magic class beside Tara and Sophia. I summoned an orb of shadow and was twirling it about in my fingers. Sophia had summoned an orb of blooming flowers and vines. Sophia worshiped the goddess of nature. Tara had summoned a flowing orb of blood, she worshipped the god of war and bloodshed. In this world who you worshipped would determine some of your magic, basically our magic would favour the god or goddess we worshipped the most and would reflect that.

Of course we could do other things with our magic like igniting candles with a snap of the fingers or set a mop to clean the floors while we are doing something else. Of course our magic had limits. It would use our own energy to power it and we would feel more and more tired the more we used it for prolonged periods of time. I looked over at the table our two fiancés were sitting at with Lord Harvey. Lord Harvey had also summoned an ord of shadows, it seems he too was a worshipper of Oiche.

Prince Edward had summoned a ball of light, he worshipped the goddess of light which was called Solas. My fiancé had summoned an orb of ice, he worshipped the goddess of the cold, Fuair. I looked at Timothy's face and saw it furrowed in concentration. We were now all seventeen years old. I didn't mean for this to happen but somehow I developed feelings for Lord Timothy. I blame the original Raven's feelings for sticking around and only surfacing when they knew they would cause the most trouble.

I thought back to what my parents had said to me when we were heading back from a ball one night years ago. "We learned to love each other" My father had told me. Back then I was stubborn and was so sure I could avoid falling in love with Lord Timothy. Well sometimes Fate didn't like to play fair. I guess I can't blame my feelings just on whatever bits of the original Raven were still inside me. I fell in love with him through these small little acts of affection over the years that he displayed to me and I guess he showed me some type of affection often enough that I started to care for him, more than I normally would for a friend.

I was unsure whether he felt the same towards, sometimes it looked like he loved me and other times he looked just like a friend looking at another friend. It was confusing to me, if this was how Lord Timothy appeared to Lady Raven in the novel then I guess I couldn't blame her for being blindsided when he announced the end of their relationship. In the book from what I remember, it has been years since I read it at this point, Lord Timothy would act cold and mean to Lady Raven for a moment and then in the nice would show her signs of affection which she so desperately craved since she didn't recieve any type of affection from her own parents. Which isn't so different to now, Marquess and Lady Darksheild both still treated their own daughter somewhat coldly and I couldn't remember ever receiving a hug from either of them.

We all looked like how we were supposed to in the novel, well expect for the way I dress, all us girls were stunning to look at for different reasons. Tara for her long red hair and captivating green eyes, Sophia for her smile which made boys stop in their tracks and do nothing but adore her. I grew to be taller than the other two girls, as it was written in the book, I had developed my father's sharp cheekbones and fearsome glare. I moved with absolute grace like my mother and no one could every find fault in my manners, just like my mother's. My parents had begun to lose hope that I would leave behind my dark clothes and wear bright colours again.

However they didn't try to force me to adhere to their expectations on what I should wear. For the most part they just let me do my own thing but would call appon me to join them for dinner or a party at the family home every once in a while and I was fine with that since I was busy with school. Surprisingly my mother had started to write me letters a year ago. I guess she missed having me around the house, in her own strange way I guess. My father doesn't wrote his own letters to me, he just adds a paragraph to mother's letter and then let's her put it in the envelope. He normally doesn't have much to say to me in his short paragraph but I could sense he did care about me, but only a little bit.

The bell rang to single the end of classes for the day. I walked back to my room in the dormitories with Sophia by my side. We were discussing about the concept of true divine magic which the teacher had been teaching us towards the end of class. Our conversation was interrupted when Lord Timothy ran up to us and grabbed hold of my elbow. "Applogies Lady Sophia I need to speak with my fiancé so I'm afraid I must take her away from you for a few moments but I promise I'll return her to you when I'm done with her!" He told Sophia quickly while dragging me away from her towards my own room.

"Okay I guess" I heard Sophia mumble sadly as she watched me being dragged away against my will by my lovebombing, overbearing fiancé. He dragged me into my room and locked the door behind us. "Let go of me at once!" I commanded furiously, how dare he treat me like that! "Come now my dear don't make that face at me, your adoring fiancé" He said when he saw me giving him a death glare which was similar to my father's death glare. He did let go of my arm though. I crossed my arms in defiance and just glared at him harder. "Raven darling come now, don't act like that!" He said softly while tugging my arms away from one another and then bring his hand up to my chin and tilted my face up. "Come on my love" He whispered almost lovingly to me "Give me a smile!".I felt like breaking his nose in that moment.

9

— • —

CHAPTER 9

I wanted to break Timothy's nose for telling me to smile after how he has treated me but my traitorous heart had other opinions on the matter. It liked seeing him like this for some sick twisted reason and so because it was so starved for any tiny bit of affection it could get it made me flash Timothy a smile. I was screaming internally at myself, why did I have to fall for this manipulative man.

Timothy presses his lips lightly against my cheekbones for the briefest of moments. It was barely even a peck on the cheek and yet it made my heart flutter. At least I won't have to deal with you for the rest of my life when you become Ashley's problem! I thought savagely in my mind as I continued to smile at Timothy. Timothy pulled me close to him and just held me in his arms for a few moments. "You wanted to talk about something Tim?" I reminded Timothy as I remembered that Sophia was probably waiting outside for me.

His face fell a bit at my words. "What can't a man just want to spend some time alone with his fiancé!" Timothy exclaimed while suddenly stepping back from me. My heart started to panic as Timothy reverted back to his usual cold self. "You can" I told him desperately as I went over to him with my arms open towards him, imploring him silently to hold me again. He regarded me for a moment, deciding whether or not to allow me to hold him. Deciding that his pride wouldn't allow for me to be the one to hold him he pulled me to him roughly. He lowered his head towards my ear and whispered "Any time we have a beautiful moment you just have to go and ruin it, don't you darling!". He pushed me away from him and my back hit my bed frame.

Timothy unlocked my door and strolled out of the room like nothing just happened. I quickly gathered myself to not let Sophia see me in such a sorry state. There was no point worrying her about what was happening in my relationship when it would be ending in a few months time.

My room at the academy wasn't much like my room back home. The academy doesn't allow us to change the rooms so the walls are a bright red and the floor was oak wood planks. We were allowed to bring our own bed sheets and curtains and other little items to make ourselves feel more at home while we are here. There is a desk with a mirror hanging above it that faced the bed. A wardrobe stood next to the bathroom door.

We all had our own private bathroom. A chest lay at the foot of my bed and it was full of books and shoes and what not else. There was a bookshelf beside the window that had a few books on it since I hadn't had the time to move all my books out of the chest and back on the bookshelf. I had my alter set up on a small coffee table beside the desk and it had my usual alter set up on it like the one I had at home.

I was sitting at my desk with an ink pen in my hand as I was finishing off the last sentence on my essay on recent politics for my political studies class. Suddenly I felt like something was watching me from the shadows underneath my bed. I carefully got up from my seat and got down on my hands and knees and put my hand into the shadows. I felt my hand hit something so I grabbed it gently and slowly pulled it out from underneath my bed. It was a rolled up scroll.

I sat cross legged on the floor and broke the wax seal on the scroll. It was a announcement from the high priest of the Temple of Oiche. There was to be a gathering in the woods beside the school tonight and worshippers of Oiche were to attend the ritual, attendance from the look of the letter was mandatory. I was to go into the woods around eight tonight and I was to wear light clothing.

I chose a short backless dress with a deep v-neck and it was of course black. The dress also had high splits in the legs that went up to mid thigh. I chose flat black shoes since it was not a good idea to wear heels in those woods unless you wanted to break your ankle. The dress also didn't have sleeves and was being held on my frame by two black thin straps. The dress wasn't form fitting and the fabric was quite loose and free flowing. Just what the letter had said to wear. Whenever a high priest refers to light clothing they mean clothing that is not modest at all, since high priests and priestesses ceremonial clothes show a lot of skin. Well for the servants of Oiche their outfits don't leave very much for the imagination.

I kept my hair down and let it flow freely since that was what rituals like thus were all about with servants of Oiche, to be able to be free in the darkness and do as we wished without the judgment we would face on the light. I painted my nails black for the occasion and wore my darkest black lipstick and eyeshadow as well. I was just about to head out the door when Timothy came barging into my room.

He was about to go off on a rant about someone who had just angered him when he saw me, more like he saw what I was wearing. "Where are you going dressed like that?" He demanded furiously, he obviously didn't approve of my outfit at all. "I am to attend a gathering in the woods tonight my love" I informed him softly while walking over to him and holding his face gently with my hands. "What's type of gathering?" He demanded to know. "Worshippers of Oiche are gathering to welcome the longer nights that are to come in the coming months as the seasons change" I explained calmly while rubbing one of his cheeks with my thumb.

He was about to say something else but I cut across him, if I answered all his questions then I wouldn't get to the gathering on time. "I must go now darling" I told him firmly while going on my tiptoes so I could give him a kiss. Timothy leaned down a bit to help me be able to reach his lips with mine. It was hard having such a big height difference. Heels usual helped close the gap between us but without them I was just about half a head shorter than him. I didn't know how Tara and Prince Edward could be bothered with kissing each other all the time.

Tara was about two heads shorter than Prince Edward and that is with her normal sized heels on. "I swear I'll explain everything when I get back" I promised him while I walked out the door. I quickly walked down the hall without looking behind me, I knew he would be leaning against the doorframe with his arms crossed like he always did when I would go off in the middle of the night and leave him behind.

10

CHAPTER 10

The air had a chill to it as I walked through the quietly slumbering forest. The moon was full tonight. As I approached the middle of the woods I could hear people quietly whispering to one another. I had found the meeting place. I heard footsteps coming from behind me and I turned around to try to see who it was. It was a tall man with long dark brown hair and silver eyes. I could just about make out his hooked nose in the dim light of the moon.

It was Lord Harvey. He was wearing a loose black shirt that had a deep v-neck along with loose fitting trousers that covered his legs that didnt show any skin. We all had different interrupatations of what the high priest wanted us to wear. "Fancy seeing you here Lady Raven!" Lord Harvey commented as he matched my pace as we walked towards the gathering. "It is a gathering to welcome the long nights why wouldn't I be here!" I spoke softly while raising one eyebrow just a tiny bit, to get a response.

"I'm just surprised that your fiancé would let you out at this time!" He told me as he stared off ahead. I chuckled "Oh if he had his way I wouldn't be here talking to you but attendance is mandatory and I wouldn't want to miss an event that the high priest of Oiche attends!". Lord Harvey chuckled and then we lapsed into silence.

Lord Harvey wasn't as bad as the novel had made him out to be. He was definitely classis but apart from that he was pleasant to talk to and truly did love and care for Lady Helena.

We stood beside each other in the small clearing, listening to the High priest preach his sermon to us before we could begin the ritual. The darkness surrounding us made it hard to see who else was there, however I could feel their presence. There was at least fourteen other worships there. All standing quietly, waiting for the High priest to give the orders for the ritual to begin.

The High priest drew his sermon to a close and then commanded us to dance. Lord Harvey took me by the hand and we began dancing in silence with the other worshipers. We twirled, leaped and danced in other ways and we did this all in nearly complete darkness without bumping into anyone. We danced for hours in the cold dark forest and only stopped because the High Priest told us to. With the ritual complete and our god of darkness contented with us we could leave the forest. The others were probably going back to their beds but I knew that I had to deal with a possibly irrated Timothy, my night was far from over.

I snuck back into the school with Lord Harvey since it was way past curfew at this point. I said goodnight to him and headed towards the girl's dormitories. I was silly enough to hope that Timothy would have returned to his own room before curfew. My hopes were dashed when I approached my room and could smell a floral candle burning. I didn't have one lit when I left. I opened my door and slipped inside.

Timothy was laying on my bed, jacket and shoes off and the top four buttons on his shirt undone. He turned his head towards me and crossed his arms, waiting for me to tell him of tonight's events. I told him I would tell him anything he wanted to know after I had bathed. I could still feel a freezing cold chill all over my body. Timothy pouted but didn't try to protest. I returned from my bathroom in a long black robe as I had forgotten to bring in my nightgown into the bathroom with me. I climbed onto my bed and laid down beside Timothy.

The floral candle was slowly flickering on my bedside table. "Arlight" I said softly "what do you want to know?". Timothy pondered for a moment. "Who was there, what you were doing and why did you have to wear that outfit in particular!" Timothy inquired. I readjusted myself on my bed and placed one of my pillows down a bug lower on my neck so my head would be supported better. "Well there was the high priest, a few other worshipers!" I told Timothy softly while trying to stiffle a yawn. "Was Harvey there?" He asked pointedly. "Yes he was there" I confirmed. He waited for me to elaborate more. "We dance underneath the moonlight for hours and then the high priest let us return home!" I elaborate.

Timothy nodded but didn't look too happy that I was dancing with another man, Timothy had a bad habit of getting jealous and suspicious too often. "So if you were just 'dancing' why did you have to wear such a scandalous outfit?" He demanded to know. I sighed "The High Priest had asked us to wear such outfits since that is what is require for the ritual to be preformed at it's best" I explained tiredly. Timothy didn't like that answer but there wasn't much he could say against it. He wasn't a part of the religion so he had no right to put his opinion on any of our practices.

Timothy and I had no major arguments over the next few weeks, mainly I was too preoccupied with worrying about the arrival of the heroine. She would make her first appearance tomorrow morning.

All my years of preparation and hard work would finally be put to the ultimate test. Maybe I should also try to befriend the heroine, to make sure I've covered all bases and possible resources to keep me from getting my head chopped off. Although just incase things don't work out I should probably write a will. It will be a really simple one. It will contain one line and that line would be NO ONE GETS ANYTHING, IF YOU TOUCH MY STUFF I WILL HAUNT YOU FOR THE REST OF YOUR LIVES!!!

11

— • —

CHAPTER 11

I paced back and forth in my room since sunrise. Today was the day. Sophia and Tara had come to my room since we usually hang around in each others rooms every morning before classes start. I needed to calm down, I couldn't let them see that something was bothering me this much. "What are you worrying so much about?" Sophia asked me.

"Oh nothing much, just the upcoming exams!" I lied. Tara was lying fully back on my bed with a book open in her hand. "I don't know what you're stressing about!" Tara drawled lazily "you always do well in exams, you are always the top of the class!". I smiled half heartedly "I know but the exams this year are the most important exams of our lives so I need to do very well in them!". Both Tara and Sophia rolled their eyes at me, they both knew without a doubt that I would ace these upcoming exams, like I always do.

We were in the dining hall, sitting at our usual table with our other friends such as Michelle, Lydia and Nina. I kept glancing towards the double wide set of doors, that was where the heroine would walk through and be presented to my year group. Any minute now and she would walk in and my life will change. I'm not sure if it will be for the better. I hadn't even considered what I would do with my life after Timothy leaves me. What was I to do after that?

Find a new husband before my parents find out and have a fit? I told myself u would worry about that after Timothy has left me. I looked away from the doors and instead quickly glanced at Helena and Harvey, they seemed so in love with one another. It was a shame that such a happy loving couple would soon break up because of the heroine. Maybe I could convince Lord Harvey to leave the heroine alone. Suddenly the doors bursted open and the headmaster walked in with a timid looking girl following behind him.

"Ladies and gentlemen may I have your attention please I have an announcement!" The headmaster declared as he walked towards the Leaving year tables. He stood in front of us while dragging the heroine by the elbow so that she stood in front of him. She was small and had short brown hair and had a small round face. She looked so small compared to the headmaster. She seemed nervous as the headmaster introduced her to us.

"This is Ashley Howl and she will be your new classmate so treat her kindly even though she is from the peasant class!" He said before taking a pause to gauge our reactions. A lot of the students at the leaving year students were shocked at her arrival, I appeared indifferent but was silently panicking inside. This was it, she had arrived and the love interests have seen her. Soon she'll begin capturing all of the love interests. I just have to survive over next few months until the end of the school year.

Ashley looked around for a bit and then decided to sit down beside Tara and me. "Hello I'm Ashley Howl!" She greeted us excitedly. "Greetings" I replied carefully while picking up my glass of water "I am Lady Raven Darksheild, the daughter of Marquess Eric

Darksheild" I introduced myself. I gave Tara a quick look to indicate she should introduce herself. "I am Lady Tara Rondish, the daughter of Duke Armin Rondish!".

Ashley seemed a bit more at ease since to her we appeared to be friendly. "So what class do you ladies have next?" She asked us sweetly, if I didn't already knew that this girl was trouble I would have fallen for the sweet and innocent act she was putting on to appear more likeable. "I have to go to social etiquette!" Tara informed her somewhat reluctantly, I presume she also felt something off about Ashley. Ashley nodded and then turned to me. "I have to go to music class" I told her while opening the morning paper that I had laying beside my plate.

The war with the neighbouring kingdom was still going on and from what the paper said it didn't look like it would end anytime soon. Prince Sebastian who is Prince Edward's older brother and is the Crown Prince of Highmooreshire is currently fighting in the war. He also doesn't have a happy ending in the novel. The war ends and Highmooreshire wins but when Prince Sebastian returns he wasn't the same as he was before. It was never really addressed in the novel but from the look of it he was suffering from PTSD and because of that he was stripped of his right to the throne and Prince Edward ascended to the throne instead. Not much is said what happened to Prince Sebastian after he lost his title of Crown Prince.

It turns out that Ashley shared all the same classes as me, the goddess of luck wasn't happy with me that day it seems. I played the organ while some of my other classmates played violins, harps, flutes and lutes. A few were singing, this included Ashley and she was a soprano. I'm a contralto which means I have a deeper singing voice which I have a low singing voice for a woman while Ashley's singing voice is high.

Ashley uses the entire class to show off how high she can sing. Everyone is in awe about her voice they claim she has a voice of an angle. I didn't let the comments bother me, it was true her voice was lovely but I shouldn't compare her voice with mine since they were so different. She may be able to reach the high noted that I can't but she can't reach the low notes that I can. Some songs would always be more suited to her voice but there would always be other songs which would go perfectly with mine.Ashley wouldn't stop pestering me with questions after music.

She wanted to know if I could sing, I told her yes and I was a contralto. She asked me how I could plan the organ so well, I told her I had been practice playing the piano since I was young and then applied myself to learn how to play the organ so I could play both instruments with artistic skill.

Ashley stuck to my side for the rest of the day and she could not stop talking even for a second. For some reason the teachers didn't tell her off for this! She finally left me alone at dinner time and I could have a few minutes of peace. As I had said before Lady Luck wasn't happy with me that day.

Timothy plopped himself down beside me and placed a baked potato with shredded cheese on top on my plate. "What's this for?" I questioned him quietly, I was suspicious since Timothy usually never gave me any of his food. It was probably poisoned or something knowing him. "Can't a man give his beloved something without being interageted like some murder!" Sighed exasperatedly.

I rolled my eyes at his dramatics and eat my dinner and made sure not to eat anything that had touched the potatoe. Timothy scoffed at my antics but I was making sure he didn't kill me now that he has saw the heroine. "I try to do one nice thing and you don't even appreciate it!" He sniffed as he pouted and gave me a face that resembled that of a sad kitten. I blinked at him and gave the potatoe back to him.

He glared at the potatoe and also didn't eat it. My presumption that something was wrong with the potatoe was right if he wasn't even interested in eating it. Timothy and I argued all the way to my room and I slammed the door in his face. He hit the door with his fist before storming off. That boy got on my nerves like no one else could, Ashley came in second. It seems that those two would be a perfect match together. Unfortunately for Timothy Ashley would leave him for Prince Edward not long after they get engaged. Oh how I'll be laughing at him when it happens!

12

CHAPTER 12

It was the weekend and I was having a lie in which I often liked to do on the weekend. Sandra had come in early and cleaned the place up a bit before leaving again. I had gotten a full hour of peace before Timothy somehow got into my room and decided to jump into bed beside me.

He had eloped me into a hug and was being very clingy for some reason. I tried to push him away at first but he held on and I got tried of trying to push him off the bed when it clearly wasn't working. "What are you doing Timothy?" I asked as he repositioned one of my pillows so that it better supported his head so he could lie more comfortably.

"Can't a man just show his fiancée some affection without being questioned all the bloody time" He said exasperatedly "What has gotten into you darling you don't normally act this bloody cold towards me!" He whined while pushing his head into the crook of my neck. "This is not appropriate Timothy, if anyone finds out you're in here with me alone there will be a scandal!" I scolded him while glancing towards the door to make sure no one would walk through it at any second and discover us. "Who's going to just walk into someone's room at eight o'clock in the morning on a Saturday morning?" Timothy said sarcastically.

Right on cue the heroine Ashley barges into my room and quickly shuts the door behind her. She appeared to be out of breath and her skirt was torn in several places. Never in my life had I seen Timothy dart away from me as fast as he did just know. Honestly if I wasn't being distracted by the sounding of someone slamming their fist on my door I would have laugh at Timothy since he had landed on face when he pushed away from me and fell out of the bed. "Open the door this instant" someone roared furiously on the other side of the door.

It was Lord Harvey banging on my door. I threw my covers off of me an grabbed my bathrobe from my bedside table and put it on. Ashley quickly turned the key in my door to lock it before Lord Harvey tried to open the door by the handle.

Ashley ran to Timothy and hid behind him. "Who the devil is that?" Timothy questioned as he made sure to hid the cowering Ashley from view. "It's Lord Harvey!" I answered as I went to unlock the door. "Don't open the door!" Ashley screeched. I ignored her and unlocked it and opened the door to reveal an irate Lord Harvey.

"Lord Harvey what brings you banging on my door at eight in the morning?" I asked Lord Harvey pointedly. His furious face softened slightly. "Applogies Lady Raven, I was not aware that this was your room!" Lord Harvey apologised sincerely. "I'm looking for Miss Howl!" He informed me while looking over at Timothy. "If you don't mind my asking but why are you currently looking for her?" I asked him while stepping back to let him into the room.

"SHE INSULTED MY FIANCÉ!" Lord Harvey accused angrily. "She insulted Helena!" I gasped in surprised. "I didn't mean any offense I swear!" Ashley squealed while still hiding behind Timothy. "How did she offend Helena?" I questioned Lord Harvey in a concerned way in which any friend would care how someone did their good friend wrong. "That little peasant deliberately did not address my fiancé correctly even after being corrected multiple times!" Lord Harvey informed the room while glaring hatefully at Ashley. I gasped but was not at all surprised at this. In the novel I vaguely remembered that Ashley got on a few people's bad sides because she was totally unaware of the social etiquette noble classes usually used.

"I'm sure she won't do it again!" I told Lord Harvey calmly in an attempt to calm him down. "She must apologise to Helena!" Lord Harvey said stubbornly. "So if Miss Howl apologies then you leave her alone and stop acting like some mad bull?" Timothy questioned Lord Harvey with this strange look in his eyes. "I will, I can swear to that!" Swore Lord Harvey.

Ashley clung to Timothy "Don't leave me alone with him!" She begged Timothy while tugging onto his arm like a child would to their father. "Don't worry I'll go with you!" Timothy comforted her while leading her out of my room. Lord Harvey and I exchanged a look, "I would advise you watch out for that one!" He warned me "She's too close to your fiancé and I have this bad feeling about that one". I nodded "I well aware Lord Harvey but I thank you for your concern!" I told him as he walked out of my room. Worried about that look Timothy gave to Lord Harvey I turned around to my wardrobe and got dressed for the day.

Tara, Sophia and I were walking through the town beside the academy as we had decided to shop that day. I had told them what happened in my room that morning and Tara was not one bit surprised. "I could tell the instant that she walked in that she was going to be trouble!" Tara told us confidently as we looked at the items on display through the shop windows. "I am a tiny bit concerned that Lord Harvey got so worked up over Miss Howl not addressing Helena the right way!" Sophia admitted.

"Why's that?" I asked Sophia carefully. Sophia moved her handbag onto her other shoulder before answering me. "Well he needs to control his temper as the way he was conducting himself isn't what is expected of a young lord but also because not everyone will address Helena correctly, especially when she becomes Lord Harvey's wife, there will be people calling her by her maiden name for a bit before they finally get it right!" Sophia explained.

Tara scoffed at Sophia's words but I nodded. "Yes he does need to learn to stop being so overprotective of Helena, it won't end well for their relationship if he doesn't give Helena a bit of space to advocate for herself " I said in reply. Tara agreed with me although she disagreed with Sophia.

We were shopping in one of the jewelers by Crawfin Street. When we saw Prince Edward walking down the street with his personal bodyguard Sir Darren, Sir Darren was only about a year older than the rest of us since he graduated from Knight Training just a few months ago. "Your Highest!" I greeted Prince Edward with a curtesy, Sophia did the same.

Tara also did a curtesy but she didn't go as far down as Sophia and I since she was Prince Edward's fiancée. "Wonderful morning isn't it ladies!" Prince Edward commented happily as his attention went from Sophia and I to Tara. I could see Tara struggling with herself to not let her slight annoyance show.

She did love Prince Edward but whenever he showed up he would take Tara with him where ever he went and we wouldn't see her again up Prince Edward had to do something that Tara couldn't come with him. Just like always Prince Edward made some small talk with us before dragging Tara off some where. Sophia and I sighed before continuing our shopping trip. When we returned to our rooms with our arms full of bags we found Ashley and Lord Timothy standing outside my room.

13

CHAPTER 13

"Hello Miss Howl!" I greeted her a bit coldly. "Hi Raven!" She greeted me happily. "Lady Raven!" Sophia corrected Ashley quickly. Ashley became embarrassed and her face turned red. Timothy rolled his eyes at Sophia, I noticed this bit kept quiet as it wouldn't do me any good with angering him this year. "So how was the situation with Helena?" I asked them while pulling my gloves further up my arms to appear nonchalant. Ashley's face brighten and her embarrassment quickly vanished.

"Oh Lady Helena was so nice and she didn't seem to mind my unintentional insult as she knew that I would struggle with all the new social etiquette I have to learn to fit in with high society!" She gushed about how kind hearted Helena was. I wasn't surprised that Helena would be able to let the little insult to her status go, she rarely held anything against anyone.

"Well I'm glad to hear that!" I told them dishonestly, I would have preferred for Helena to treat Ashley more coldly but I had to remind myself. Not all of us are destined to be the villains in this story and anyway Lord Harvey will hold this transgression against Ashley even though Helena has forgiven her. That was just the sort of person he was.

"I'm guessing you been by Miss Howl's side since this morning" I said to Timothy with slight accusation in my voice. Timothy turned to me and the look in his eyes were cold. "I was, do you have some sort of problem with that?" He questioned me, his tone challenging me to say I did.

I thought briefly about giving into my jealously but that is what the prevention Lady Raven did in this situation and she had argued with Timothy and this caused more strain on their relationship and made Timothy more resentful of Lady Raven since she accused him of a lot of things that didn't happen. I took a deep breathe and tried my very best at pushing the feelings of jealously that were clawing their way into my chest.

"No" I said simply "I was just curious of what you've been up to since the last time I saw you!". Ashley looked a bit surprised at my response, I hazarded a guess that she was expecting a bigger reaction from me. Timothy also looked a bit surprised that I currently wasn't screaming at me but he seemed happy by this result. "Now if you'll excuse us I promised Miss Howl a personal tour of the academy!" Timothy informed Sophia and I while dragging Ashley away from us.

Ashley looked at me with this strange look I couldn't decipher and an uneasy feeling started prickling at the back of my neck. "Well aren't they strange!" Sophia commented snidely, I nodded in agreement "That girl is trouble for sure!" Sophia went on as I opened the door to my room.

It was early on Sunday morning and I was getting ready to head to the temple service. Sarah was moving about my room trying to find some jewelry that I had misplaced. "Well i don't have the foggiest idea where you onyx earings have gone m'lady!" Sarah stated tiredly as she slowly stood up.

"That's all right Sarah" I told her while putting on my necklace with a circle of obsidian on the centre of it "I'm sure I'll find them eventually, don't work yourself up over it, I'll live without them!". I was wearing a long flowing black dress with a tight dark grey corset and black heeled boots. I has grey eyeshadow with black sharp winged eyeliner on along with black lipstick. I had put my hair into a tight fish braid that reach the base of my back. I grabbed one my long black clocks while grabbing my purse with my other hand. "Right see you later Sarah!" I said as I walked out the door.

I was walking out of the front entrance of the academy and saw Helena and Lord Harvey not far ahead of me. I quickened my pace to catch up with them. They seemed to be in a world of their own as they didn't notice me approaching then and they still didn't notice me as we walked all the way to the temple district. Lord Harvey had walked over with Helena to the Temple of the god of love, Grá. He planted a kiss on her palm before walking off towards the temple of Oiche. I went with him.

The temple of Oiche was made from obsidian pillars and onyx titles and the insides were dimly lit. It is important to note that the temple of Oiche was also the temple of Cogadh, the god of war and bloodshed. This is because the royal family a couple hundred years ago didn't want to give evil gods their own temples so they would often group two or three evil gods in the same temple to discourage people from worshipping them due to the cramp conditions inside since the temples for the evil gods were usually a lot smaller than the temples for the good or neutral gods like Grá and Fuair.

"Greetings Lady Raven" Lord Harvey greeted me quickly, "Greetings to you as well Lord Harvey!" I replied in a similar manner. "Your fiancé seems to be quite good 'pals' with that Howl girl!" Lord Harvey remarked. I could tell from how he said the word pals that he thought they were more than that. "Yes" I mused "they do seem to be getting a long rather well". I felt my heart ache from jealously and hurt.

Obviously I should have been prepared for this, knowing he is with someone else behind my back, the comments people will make to me about seeing them together so much. Preparing for something and actually living through it is two very different things. No amount of preparing could prepare me for this.

The inside of the temple had skulls on tables that were covered with dark bloodstained table cloths. The skulls had candles sticking our of their eye sockets. I could see a few knives embedded into the walls from past fights. Lord Harvey and I walked side by side to the temple sanctuary which the service was to be held in.

The high priest of Oiche was standing outside of the door to the sanctuary, greeting people as they walked in. "It is good to see you again Lord Shineblade!" The high priest greeted Lord Harvey with a handshake. "It is wonderful to see you here again Lady Darksheild!" He smiled with an attractive grin. I bowed my head to him in response and walked past him to go sit beside Lord Harvey since he was the only one in my year who worshipped Oiche. On the other side of the sanctuary I saw a head of long red hair wearing a long red dress. It was Tara, I tipped my head in her direction and she tipped her head in acknowledgement before bowing her head in prayer.

14

CHAPTER 14

It was nearing midnight and I was on top of the academy, I was on the roof and was far from my room where I should have been. I wasn't dressed for the weather in any way. I was wearing my lightweight and sheer grey nightgown but I had my long black satin robe over the top of it. Even in this life I couldn't escape every bad habit I had in my old life, one of those I couldn't fully escape from was smoking.

Not anything drug related just tobacco. In this world they had cigars and small thin cigarettes like they did in the eighteen hundreds in my original world. I pressed the light cigarette to my lips and filled my lungs with the dark smoke. At least in this world smoking didn't have negative side effects like they did in the other world. You couldn't get terribly sick from them but if you smoked them too much you could suffer from seeing things that aren't actually there. I heard footsteps coming from behind me and I turned around to see who it was.

It was Lord Harvey. "Fancy seeing you here Lady Raven!" Lord Harvey quipped as he sat down beside me on the roof. "I could say the same to you" I replied while taking a drag from the cigarette in-between my fingers. Lord Harvey leaned back and looked at me and the cigarette I had placed against my lips. "I didn't realise you smoked as well!" He commented while putting his hands behind his head so he could look up at the stars comfortably.

"Would you like one Lord Harvey?" I asked him while tugging the tin case I kept my cigarettes in out of the pocket on my robe. "I would!" He said as he took one of them from the tin "and please call me Harvey we've known each other long enough!". I chuckled "then you'll have to call me Raven then". "That I would Raven" He said as he lit the cigarette and drew in a lung full of smoke.

We sat up on that roof smoking for a few minutes before we got bored of looking at the landscape. "What to go explore the woods?" Harvey inquired as he put out his cigarette on the roof tile beside him. I laughed "The woods?" I thought he lacked sense in that moment "Neither of us is dressed for such an adventure!" I stated while gesturing to our clothes.

I was in a sheet nightgown and robe with flat leather shoes and Harvey had long silk bed trousers and leather boots and a light grey cotton t-shirt on. Harvey flashed me a smile, "Oh come Raven live a little" He teased "We're only going to be in this school for only a few months more so why not explore what we can while we still have time!". I sighed "Fine but we're not going very far in!".

We climbed down from the roof and started heading towards the woods. The moon's light provided us a little light to find our way through the darkness that surrounded us. Harvey led me through the forest as he wanted to show me something. It was cleared he had been to the part of the forest he wanted to explore before.

I should have felt uneasy about this but for some unexplainable reason I trusted him and we with him happily. We emerged from the trees into a small open space with a large rock in the middle of it.

Around the rock were candles that were already lit. I thought this was strange and was worried for a moment that Harvey was going to sacrifice me in some sort of ritual when he pulled me into the bushes and told me to stay quiet. Confused but wanting to see what was going to happen I stayed quiet and waited.

I heard rustling coming from infront of us and Sir Darren appeared, he wasn't in his suit of armour and Prince Edward was no where to be seen. He was alone for the moment. Harvey look at me and gave me this mischievous look. "Sorry about this!" He whispered menacingly before pushing me out of the bush. I was fully prepared to start cursing at him when Sir Darren rushed over to me. "Are you alright Lady Raven?" He asked me in a concerned tone while offering me his hand to help me off the ground.

"I am no need to worry!" I said flustered, being pushed out of the bush had undid the ribbon around my robe and now some of the nightgown was on show and Sir Darren clearly saw more than he wanted too as he look away, also flustered. For the record the gown was only sheer at the side of my thighs and a little bit over my shoulders but of course to knights and noble men even showing a bit of ankle was seen as immodest so me with most of my legs on show was more than what Sir Darren had ever seen before."If you don't mind my asking M'lady but why by the divine are you out in the last month of autumn in the middle of the night in very little clothing?"

He asked as he looked away as I quickly retied the ribbon on my robe, never in my life had I been so embarrassed than I was then. "I was walking around the place as you do" I lied quickly hoping he would buy it and not as me anymore questions. "Yes but why wear such indecent clothing when the weather is getting colder?"

He questioned me as he presumed I was alone and he probably thought at this point I was crazy or stupid, probably a bit of both at that point.

"Oh I was meeting someone!" I lied nonchalantly hoping he would lose interest in questioning me. "With who I see no one but us around?" He interagated me. "I've already met up with them!" I explained quickly hoping Harvey had enough sense to get away from here before Sir Darren could assume it was him I've been "meeting". Sir Darren looked at me with a skeptical look. "Are you not already promised to Lord Timothy Bainne?".

"I am!" I answered carefully, I could see where this was going and was silently cursing myself for not thinking of another lie that wouldn't get me in trouble with Timothy if Sir Darren told him about this. "Then tell me why you are meeting someone dress like that when you are supposed to be marrying another!" He growled at me. I took a step back, Sir Darren was known in the novel to be hot headed and harsh and not someone you wanted to anger, he also notably despised adulterers as the first woman he courted cheated on him with one of his squad mates.

"Before you jump to conclusions I wasn't meeting them for anything scandalis" I explained quickly as I tried to fix my mistakes "It was an emergency and I was already in my nightwear so I ran out of my room to meet her since it was so urgent!". I added in the little bit of information that I was meeting a girl since I remembered one other aspect of Sor Darren's character, he didn't know that people could love someone of the same gender as them, he didn't know people who liked the same gender existed because no one had ever told him and he had never encountered people who were homosexual so it would make the most sense that he wouldn't expect anything indecent happening when I told him I was meeting with a girl.

I couldn't understand how he made it this far in life without knowing that some people were homosexual, the temple of Grá had a few same sex couples worshiping in the temple every week and I knew that Sir Darren attended the temple beside it due to him worshiping the god of loyalty and leadership so I couldn't understand how he never realised it was a thing. Either way I was thankful his ignorance towards the subject of love would allow me to get out of this tricky situation. After a bit more back and forth Sir Darren finally didn't expect me to be cheating on my fiancé, I needed to tell Sophia when I see her in the morning that if Sir Darren asks I was with her because she had an emergency and needed my help for something.

I do hope she wouldn't be annoyed with me. Sir Darren insisted on walking me back and out of the corner of my eye I saw Harvey laughing quietly at me, I scrunched my nose at him but quickly went back to looking straight ahead. The last thing I needed was for Sir Darren to see Harvey who was also wearing something that would be considered inappropriate for the woods and then accusing us of cheating on our betrothed with each other. If Sor Darren ever told Timothy he met me tonight I was never going to hear the end of it from Timothy.

CHAPTER 15

Winter has arrived and soon would be the academy's Winter Games. The Winter Games are challenges made by the headmaster and you have to use magic and your intelligence and wisdom to be able to make it through the Games unharmed. From what I remembered from the novel it isn't the heroine who wins, however I couldn't remember who wins it which would have been very useful for me to remember right now but it has been years since I've actually read the novel.

I couldn't remember if Lady Raven played a huge role in the games but that doesn't really matter since I think that she doesn't interact much with Ashley during the Games. I was in magic class when the headmaster strolled in with a big leather bound book in his arms. "Good evening Ladies and Gentlemen as you all know the annual Winter Games are to commence within two weeks time" He explained to us while untying the ribbon that was wrapped around the book.

Ashley was sitting in the seat that Harvey usually sat in and because Harvey was receiving death glares from Prince Edward and Timothy he had decided to sit in between Tara and I. Sophia being the team player that she is was giving Ashley a dirty look every once in a while to show what she thought of her. I had made sure to inform Sophia of last night's events and she is on board with it. Timothy hasn't seemed to have heard about my late night outing as he hasn't confronted me about it yet which I guess is good for me.

"You all will be divided into teams of four!" The headmaster announced to us as he looked down at the list of names in his book. Each time was named after an animal and the team would have to face challenges that corresponded with that animal. "On the Wolf Team will be Lady Raven Darksheild, Lord Harvey Shineblade, Lady Sophia Clarnish and Lady Tara Rondish!". I had to stop myself from snorting, of course all of the novel's antagonists and their friend would be put on the same team.

"On the Turtledove Team will be his royal highest, the second Prince of Highmooreshire, Prince Edward Stormbrood!" The head-master announced and bowed to Prince Edward ad he was suppose to as was in line with the etiquette of this world. "Lord Timothy Bainne will also be on the Turtledove Team along with Ashley Howl and Lady Helena Stems!". I glanced at my friend's and saw that Harvey looked crestfallen at not being in the same team as the love of his life. If looks could kill then Tara would have murdered Ashley the second it was announced that Ashley and Prince Edward would be on the same team.

"I will kill that no good peasant" Tara growled softly while gripping her pen so hard I thought it would burst from the pressure. I leaned discreetly over the table and took the pen from her before she could burst it. "Now now Tara" I whispered consoling while the headmaster read out the other names on the list.

"You can't kill her as that could get you in trouble". Tara clenched her jaw and sighed aggravativly through her nostrils. "However" I added slyly "that doesn't mean that you can't damage her face during the Games!". Tara smiled wickedly at my words she approved. It appeared that the Tara I had known all these years wasn't as sweet or not as bloodthirsty as I previously thought, turns out I hadn't seen her when she felt threatened by another woman so close to her fiancé.

Even Harvey approved "That Raven is a brilliant idea" He whispered softly into my ear as I was still halfly leaning over him as I had to lean across him to get to Tara. My ear was directly infront of his mouth so he didn't have to speak very loudly for me to hear him.

The only person who had a problem with my suggestion on the wolf team was Sophia. Turns out she isn't a fan of injuring people who have gotten on our bad sides. "Miss Howl has done nothing to you all why by the divine do you want to hurt her?" She questioned us. "She's trying to steal our fiancées away from us!" Tara growled furiously.

"Not Harvey's!" Sophia reasoned, "She may not be after Helena but she is trying to turn her against me!" Harvey told us. "How?" I asked Harvey as this was the first I was hearing of this. Harvey sighed before readjusting himself in the seat before answering me. "She's been telling Helena I've been threatening her and what not!" He informed us. "Have you been threatening her?" Sophia inquired as we all knew that Harvey held grudges and was quick to become anger. "I haven't I swear!" He swore to us.

Sophia still wasn't okay with the plan so I had to come up with a way to reassure her. "Look we won't mortally wound her" I reassured Sophia "We just want to send a message to her!". Sophia looked at me skepticly, "What sort of message?" She asked. "One that says to stay away from our fiancées!" Tara interjected and I could tell from her tone that she would have added in a few swear words if she could but that wasn't allowed in the academy. They had put a ward up that could detect if someone cursed/swore since the headmaster didn't want people saying anything blasphemous or anything not civil and polite. Sophia still wasn't fully on board with the idea but she would stop us if we did.

I was pouring over some spell books in my room when I realised, I just organised a plan to harm the heroine which is something a villainess would do. My heart started to race, what if my fate was unavoidable? What if I put all this effort in for nothing? I shook my head to get rid of the unsettling thoughts, I mustn't think that.

I was going to survive, I had to.It seems like some things I couldn't change, Lord Harvey and Lady Tara wanted to bring about Ashley's downfall in some way because she got on the wrong side of them. I didn't care that she was stealing Timothy from me, even though it made my heart ache at the thought of it, I knew from the start of this that he wasn't mine to keep but still my traitorous heart had to have fallen in love with him.

I still blame the original Lady Raven's feelings for that happening. I just had to wonder what I should do about the Timothy situation, I wonder if his relationship with Ashley is developing enough that he'll want to leave me but won't out of duty to his father who worked hard in convincing my father to let Timothy marry me. I closed the book I had on my lap and got off my bed and went towards the window and stared out at the academy grounds. I couldn't help but think about the signs I needed to watch out for to determine when Timothy would break off the engagement with me. He would be rather short in talking with me and he wouldn't come visit me as often as he once had. He would also spend a lot of time with her and would hate spending any amount of time with me.

As I stared off into space, overthinking the challenges that were to come that had nothing to do with the upcoming winter games, the door to my room open and Timothy walked in. "Hello Darling!" He said in greeting while closing the door behind him and locking it.

16

CHAPTER 16

"Hello Darling!" He said in greeting as he closed the door behind him while locking it. "Hello" I said rather weakly in reply. I could see Timothy's reaction in the glass, he was surprised. Normally I would be more estatic with my greeting to him but my greeting was anything but warm and welcoming. "Is something the matter darling?" He asked me while he walked over to my bed and picked up one of the books I had on it. "Oh not much just thinking" I told him with a sigh, I kept my gaze firmly towards the window.

"And what would you be worrying about so much?" He asked me while sitting down on my bed while opening the book to the page I had marked to remember my place "you haven't been your usual self lately!, what's been bothering you so much?". I moved my tongue across my teeth as I thought of my reply, how could I word how have I been feeling to him without making it seem that I was putting the blame on Ashley as he would no doubt defend her and demonise me.

I wasn't answering Timothy quickly enough for his liking so he began pressuring me to tell him what was wrong with me. "Darling if something is bothering you you know you can tell me I'm sure we could solve the problem together!" He told me while he walked up behind me and put his hands on my shoulders while whispering in my ear.

"You won't like what's been bothering me!" I told him quietly. He chuckled softly, "Come now darling" He whispered in a reassuring way "whatever it is I'm sure I can handle it so just tell me!". I tore my gaze away from the window and turned my head and looked Timothy in his eyes "I can no longer bare to see you like this!" He added dramatically. I sighed sadly knowing what I was about to say was going to set off his anger.

"You would tell me you wanted to leave me and be with someone else right?" I asked him quietly and wishing almost immediately I had just kept my mouth shut. Timothy looked taken back for a moment and then looked slightly angry and offended. "What in the world have I done to make you question my loyalty to you?" He asked me while turning me around so that I faced him fully.

"Who has been saying horrible things about me that would have put doubt into your head that I would love anyone but you?" He questioned me fiercely while shaking me by my shoulders. "You are hurting me!" I told him firmly while trying to pry his fingers off of my shoulders that were being to dig into them. He quickly took his hands off of me and began to pace about the room while going off on a rant.

I let him have his rant, and while waiting for him to finish it got me thinking. Did I really want to endure the next few months like this, constantly questioning his alteratior motives and if the heroine had finally captured his heart. I knew I couldn't do this for any longer, it wouldn't belong before the situation would escalate and I wasn't going to put myself through that. "I want to end the engagement!" I announced firmly while crossing my arms and heading towards the door. Timothy stopped in his tracks and just stared at me with his mouth half open.

"Excuse me what!" He exclaimed. "I want to end the engagement!" I repeated again but slowly this time while dragging our the words to emphasise them. Words failed him for a moment but then he responded "No you can't!" He said in an undignified tone. "If I want this to end then I can!" I retired and crossed my arms angrily.

He looked like he was about to have a hissy fit but thought better of it. "Don't you dare even think about leaving me!" He threatened me "and just wait till I tell my father about this!". "Go ahead!" I said cooky while stomping over towards my door and opening it, indicating that Timothy had overstayed his welcome. Timothy stormed out of my room and slammed the door behind him. I knew that there was going to be a price to pay for all of this but if it got me away from him then it would be worth it.

It didn't take long for me to recieve a letter from my parents, they were ordering me to come to the family home the following Sunday. They were planning an intervention for Timothy and I's engagement. They didn't want it to end, complete ignoring my feelings on the matter. I would have to convince them when I met up with them on Sunday, I did not plan to be subjected to Timothy's mistreatment any longer.

Timothy and I didn't speak at all during the week. Ashley was always comforting Timothy whenever I saw him and I didn't care. She would have him soon anyways and she could keep him. However since I plan to survive and not get killed by Timothy I would have to put up with Timothy trying to crawl back to me.

Knowing that my parents approve of Timothy being a suitable love match for me they would no doubt pressure me into taking him back but I wasn't going to do that no matter what. I had better things to do than have to deal with an unstable Timothy. My friends noticed the rift between Timothy and I, Tara and Harvey were concerned since they thought Timothy and I had a good relationship. Sophia was delighted with me and Timothy growing apart, she never liked him and she always told me that he gave off this bad vibe.

At least now that I wasn't being bothered by Timothy for attention I found that I had a lot more focus and I was able to plot more plans for the winter games. I let the others review them and Sophia would edit the plans here and there if she felt that they went too far or were unachievable. We were just planning against Ashley, we also had to plan how to win the games and I wanted to win since there was going to be this huge prize for the winning team. The winning team would get to go to an undisclosed ancient temple and get to explore it and get to keep any artifacts they might find as long as it didn't concern King Farrow, the king of Highmooreshire. The novel never said what artifacts were in the temple so I wanted to see for myself what this ancient mystical temple had to offer.

From what the local newspaper have been saying there looked to be signs that the war between the kingdom's of Highmooreshire and Clarnish would come to an end within the next year. Since I already read the novel I knew that the war would end around the same time that Ashley had won Prince Edward's heart.

Right now Tara and Prince Edward had been having a few lovers quarrels but they would always make up quickly so it seems that Ashley hasn't influenced Prince Edward much yet since she is focusing on Timothy but I knew that sooner or later she would go after Prince Edward and leave Timothy in the dust with a heart broken Sir

Darren since she would also capture his heart and break it into tiny pieces since she would choose the Prince over his bodyguard.

I would be there for Tara and held her through the break-up and keep her from doing anything drastic. Harvey and Helena on the other hand, their relationship seems to still be going strong but cracks were starting to appear. I would need to keep an eye on those to and intervene if the need arose. I would also stop Harvey retaliating whenever Ashley would start whispering things into Helena's ear. I didn't have to worry about Sophia as she would be just fine and I knew she would help me keep the other two in check to make sure we all survive the school year and get to graduate.

17

CHAPTER 17

I wouldn't attend the dinner my parents had set up to fix my engagement. It had to be rescheduled since the headmaster declared that the winter games were moved forward and would begin on Saturday. Currently it is Friday morning and just five minutes after the headmaster had announced this. First was panic, my parents would be furious and i was panicking since there was still so much my friends and I had to prepare for. Not just for the games but also for the Winter Ball that would be held at the Royal Palace in honor of the winners. Prince Sebastian would also be there but only briefly since he had a war to get back to.

We had six hours to prepare before we would be thrown into the fighting arena. The arena was a closed off space filled with forest area and rivers. We had to complete challenges to win. Whoever finished their challenges first would win. The wolf team had decided to sabotage the turtle dove team while we completed our own challenges.

I was wrapping my knuckles in a bandaged to prevent them from getting damaged if I needed to punch something when Timothy walked into my room without even knocking. "Out!" I commanded at once. Timothy stood definently, "No!" He replied childishly. I stopped doing what I was doing for a moment and looked up at him. "Get out you're not welcome here!" I told him firmly. "We need to talk!" He stated calmly, I got off my bed and walked over to my dresser in the corner of my room. "I don't have time for that right now, we'll talk after the games!" I informed him while tying my long hair into two braids and then making a milk maids braid hairstyle to keep my hair out of my way.

"I see no reason why we can't discuss our future at this very moment!" He retorted stubbornly, I rolled my eyes in annoyance. I turned around in sharply and crossed my arms in anger. "Look Tim I don't have time for whatever it is you're trying to do right so whatever you're trying to do pack it in and leave me alone!" I growled furiously at him, my nerves were at their limits, I was nervous and Timothy annoying me like this was aggravating me a lot. "I am trying to save our relationship since you so desperately want to end it!" He shouted at me "You aren't even attempting to fix this, fix us, some days I wonder whether you ever loved me at all!".

My patience snapped, "I have loved you since the very beginning!" I screamed "You never cared for me!" Tears were beginning to fall from my eyes and run down my cheeks, running my mascara and eyeliner as I desperately tried to wipe them away. "You were always so cruel to me when we first met, and even after all these years you still haven't figure out how to treat me right!". "I do treat you right!" He interrupted me incredulously. "No you bloody don't!" I shouted at him before moving past him and running out the door, I shove him on my way out.

I agreed to meet with my friends to go over the strategy one last time before the games began. I arrived in one of the parlors that students were allowed to congregate in. I had made a quick detour to the lavatory to wash the makeup off my face, it was ruined and there was no way I could salvage it. At least no one could chastise me for not wearing makeup since the games would have wrecked it anyway, at least I wouldn't have smeared makeup all over my face at the end of the games like some people would. My friends were sitting at the sofas and I joined them.

Tara chose to forgo makeup as well, Sophia had very minimal makeup which was alright since she didn't have to do anything very labour intensive like me, Tara and Harvey would be doing. She would be there to summon plants to help us if we engage in battle since she can summon these great enormous vines that can bear people's weight and be able to throw or restrain them. Harvey had his long brown hair tied into a bun at the base of his neck, Tara had hers in a braid that wrapped around her head in a way that a crown would be worn. Sophia had her hair up in a ponytail. We went over the plan one final time before everything went dark and silent for a moment. Next thing I saw was that we were lying on the ground beside a river and the headmaster's voice was ringing out all around us.

"Welcome to the Winter Games Ladies and Gentlemen!" The Headmaster's voice announced "You will have one day to complete the tasks in this area before you will be rescued from the arena, remember you most complete the tasks first to win!"I got myself off the ground and looked around me. There was a patch of trees over by my right and a river rapids on my left. "Remember students there is to be no killing other students in these games, we are far more civilised than those Clarnishians!" The Headmaster declared before his voice left.

I helped Sophia to stand up while Harvey helped Tara off the ground. We were all dress in black skin tight suits with a white scarf wrapped around our necks. These were what we were given to wear as part of the wolf team. Harvey surveyed the area for a moment and in no time at all found the roll if parchment with our first task. He always had very good eyesight.

Winter has arrived and so has the snow, Your garments are not suitable for the weather, therefore find the fur coats to continue onto your next challenge!

We looked at the task, the first task is always the simplest to understand, we had to find fur coats. It shouldn't be the most difficult since it's the first task of the games. "Where should we start?" Tara asked quietly as she had already begun to suspect that other people couldn't be far away from us and could try to sabotage us like we would do to them. "That patch of trees over there!" Harvey said while indicating to the trees on our right.

"They are not there, the nature there doesn't have anything unusual around it!" Sophia told us while using her plant magic to see if the coats were there before we would begin looking for them. "Then where do you suggest we look?" I asked her while looking around me for any hint of something that didn't belong to nature naturally. I saw something black in the river, it was a large square thing that looked to be made out of cloth. "Their in the river!" I stated quickly while rushing to collect them. I plunged my hands into the icy cold water and yanked the cloth wrapped bundle out of the river. I threw the water proof cloth off of the bundle and saw four neatly packed black fur coats. We all grabbed one and put them on. Just in time to as it began to snow.

18

—— ● ——

CHAPTER 18

After we put on the coats I went to pick up the water proof cloth since we could use it to shield ourselves from the falling snow and prevent us from getting wet. I saw something has been stuck to the inside of the cloth. It was a bit of parchment. I carefully took the parchment and slowly pulled it off the cloth since it had been applied to the cloth with glue, there is no such thing as tape in this world. After taking the parchment carefully off the cloth without ripping it I read it allowed to the others.

A hare with a collar of leaves and berries is running amach in the forest,to progress to your next quest you must catch the hare with the collar of leaves and berries and figure out the riddle it has!

"So we have to find a hare with a wreath around its neck?" I said in a slight questioning tone. 'Seems so!" Harvey replied as he took the paper from me and read it himself. We headed off towards the forest since that is where the parchment said to go to find the hare. The further we went in the darker our surroundings became. Harvey and I were the most comfortable in our dark surroundings, Tara was holding onto Harvey by the sleeve of his coat and I was guiding Sophia through the darkest by holding her hand and pulling her behind me as I navigated us through the forest.

"How are we meant to find this bloody hare!" Tara growled furiously as she nearly tripped over another rock. "We just have to walk around until we bump into it!" Sophia said to Tara as I stopped her from walking face first into a tree. "It would make more sense for us to hunt it!" Harvey commented seriously "it would take too long for us to wander aimlessly in the hope of finding one creature!". I agreed with Harvey, we weren't making much progress as we were.

We decided to split up at this point, Tara and Sophia would go scouting to figure out how the other teams were doing while Harvey and I would go hunt for the hare since it seems that only him and I could see clearly enough in the dark to actually recognise things. We would meet back up at the river we started at once we finished.Harvey and I went deeper into the forest while discussing in low voices about how we would catch the hare. Harvey suggested that if we found it we should throw a few rocks at it to kill it so we wouldn't have to run after it. I didn't quite like that plan, we could ruin the riddle that way and the paper said that the hare would give us a riddle so we could need to keep the hare alive to get the riddle. In the end we decided to send a few creatures of darkness to ensnare the hare when we caught sight of it.

We managed to make our way to a clearing and we stopped in our tracks. There sitting on a rock was a hare with a wreath around its neck. Harvey was about to summon some shadows when the hare ran off speedily. In an instant I raced after it while summoning my own creatures and sent them ahead of me. I maneuvered my way around the trees and bushes and jumped over fallen logs in my path. Harvey wasn't far behind me but the hare was still in the lead of our little race. I could see that the rabbit was heading for a dead end.

We were coming close to the wall in the area. It seems that we were in one of the corners so all we had to do was block its path away from us. Luckily we didn't have to throw ourselves on the ground to grab the hare. It seems the hare wasn't as good at seeing in the dark as us since it ran head first into the corner and knocked itself out instantly. Honestly for a second I was worried it had killed itself since it hit itself on the head very hard. Luckily it was alive as we confirmed it was breathing. I scooped the hare into my arms and Harvey and I made our way out of the forest. Harvey sent the creatures of darkness away as we emerged from the forest. The sun was setting but at least Tara and Sophia were sitting by the river bank waiting for us.

Seek some grass,For what you need is glassFind the sphere,Before those who you hold dearFind the bone,Before the old crone

We managed to bring the hare back to consciousness, I was correct, the hare would tell us the riddle so if we had killed it like Harvey wanted to we would have never been able to proceed in the games. However, we were a bit stuck on the actual riddle itself. The first line was easy, we would have to go to an area with a lot of grass and find something made from glass.Tara had commented that she thought that the first four lines fit together and we would have to find a crystal ball. I listened to the fourth line again. "Before those you hold dear", did the turtle dove team have to find the same thing as us?

Harvey had said earlier before the games that they would likely pit is against each other so that they wouldn't have to make a lot of different challenges and this was some of the teams wouldn't be able to complete their challenges so it would be easier to tell who the winners of the winter games were.We were unsure if we had go take the hare with us but Sophia scooped the adorable hare into her arms and told us point blank that he was coming with us. None of us wanting to argue with her and knowing we may need the hare to recite the riddle again we let the hare join us while we went off in search of a large patch of grass.

I asked Tara if Sophia and her were successful in scouting out the other teams. She told me they were. I asked her how far the turtle doves were in their challenges. Tara informed me that they looked to be one challenge ahead of us and since there was four challenges we had to complete it would make sense that their last challenge would intertwine with our second last challenge. We would be what would hold them back from winning. "Do you think that the faculty step this up since they know that we care about our fiancées dearly and we would struggle with being the reason they wouldn't win?" I questioned softly. "They may have!" Tara responded while turning her head in different directions to make sure we weren't missing something made from glass in the grass.

Night had fallen and we were about to take a break since we had been walking for hours at this point when I wasn't watching my feet and tripped over something. What was the point at being able to see in the dark when I didn't watch where I was putting my feet. "Are you injured?" Harvey asked me while snickering. "I am no need to rush to help me up!" I said sarcastically while picking myself up while the others were trying hard not to laugh at my own foolishness. I looked down at what I had tripped on and found a ball made from glass beside my foot. "Found the glass and the sphere!" I announced as I grabbed the ball and held it out in front of me."Excellent, now all we need is a bone!" Harvey said while taking the ball from me and tucking it into one of the inside pockets of his fur coat. Like many clothing items the men's clothing had bigger and deeper pockets than the woman's.

19

CHAPTER 19

Inspired by our new-found luck we decided to forgo our break and ran off in search of the bone from the riddle. We decided to head back into the forest and so far we hadn't encountered anyone else while searching for the things we needed which was strange.

The area wasn't that big so we should have bumped into someone by now. Now the forest was pitch-black and we had to keep Tara and Sophia in front of us to make sure we didn't lose them. "Is it weird or has anyone else noticed the absence of other people?" I asked the group, Harvey nodded in agreement.

"Oh most of the other teams have injured themselves doing foolish things so they had to be taken out early!" Sophia informed us and Tara nodded in conformation. "Who's left then?" Harry inquired with Tara and Sophia. "Our team and the turtle doves!" They answered. I groaned, of course it would be between us and them. I was hanging onto the hope that even if we didn't win at least some other team would.

At least I could get a few hits at Ashley since most likely we will be brawling with each other to claim ownership over the glass ball. I wasn't sure whether we would also have to fight them over the bone but from what the riddle said we had to find it before the "old crone" so must likely we would be fighting an old woman for it. A part of me felt that it was a bit unfair towards the old woman but I had to remind myself that they wouldn't put an old non-magical woman into the winter games to fight some magical teenagers, we would win this fight by the scrape of our teeth or the old woman would destroy us because most likely they would have gotten some very power old woman who didn't have much else going on to fight us just to knock us down a peg or two.

We came across an old abandoned cottage in the middle of the forest. It was covered in vines and moss. Sophia moved her hand over the vines and they retracted out of sight. Harvey kicked open the door and we all ventured inside. It was dark which wasn't a problem for Harvey and I but Tara and Sophia still couldn't see very well in the dark. Tara held her hand out in front of her and used her magic to feel around for a candle or a fire place. She flicked her wrist and the wick of the candle that lay on an old battered table ignited, casting a small amount of light onto the table. The light reflected slightly off the pearly white bone which looked like it had been polished not too long ago. We presumed that this was the bone that we were meant to take. I was about to grab it when a door that lead to another room in the cottage bursted open and a hag came storming out. It was a night hag which meant she was at her most powerful at night, which was unfortunately what the time was then.

I snatched the bone from the table and jumped back to position myself in-between my friends. The night hag casted a force field spell which barricaded us in the cottage. "Give me that bone little girl!" The night hag snarled at me while entering one long boney hand towards me while her palm was facing upwards, indicating

I should hand the bone over to her. "No I won't!" I stated firmly while quickly stuffing the bone into my coat. The night hag smiled menacingly "oh you'll regret that little girl!". The hag took the staff in her hand and banged the bottom of it on the ground. The flame on the candle extinguished and we were plunged into darkness. The hag probably presumed that we couldn't see in the dark as well as she could, she was half right as only two of us could see in the dark. It would mostly be up to Harvey and I to fight the night hag while Tara and Sophia provided us with support or they could find a way to break the force field surrounding the dilapidated cottage.

Sophia and Tara moved back towards the front door since the force field provided just enough light for them to find their way towards the door. Harvey and I moved back towards the door to protect Tara and Sophia from the night hag. The hag twirled her staff and pointed it at Harvey since he was closer to her. Harvey was thrown backwards and his back slammed against the wall. I moved right hand in a circle before flicking it at the hag. Tentacles made from shadows erupted from the ground and ensnared the hag by her ankles and the tentacles also grabbed hold of the staff to prevent the hag from producing for spells from it. "You naughty insolent child I'll have your head for this!" The hag screeched in fury. I could hear a few people shouting behind me but they sounded far off like something was blocking them.

I didn't dare take my eyes off the hag. The hag clicked her fingers and a ball of fire came hurdling towards me, I threw myself to the ground to the right to avoiding getting hit. I twisted my wrist and the tentacles slowly started climbing their way up the hag and the staff. They were going to restrain her but the staff started to emit this blinding white light.

I covered my eyes to prevent getting blinded and tried to get back up to my feet quickly. The light would have disemtagrated the shadow tentacles so the hag would be freed within seconds. I sprinted over to where Harvey was trying to pick himself up from the floor while covering his eyes with his sleeve. The light vanished and the hag was indeed freed and was irate at this point. I grabbed Harvey by his and and pulled him up. Harvey quickly summoned an orb of shadow and hurled it at the hag, it hit her directly in the face. The shadows burst and formed a tight mask around the hag's face. I once again called the shadow tentacles but this time once the shadows had ensnared the hag I grabbed her staff and threw it into the room she came out of. Harvey casted his own force field but not as magnificent as the hag's one.

Harvey's force field encircled the hag and Harvey made it strong enough to keep the hag at bay for a few minutes while we escaped. The hag clawed desperately at the mask that surrounded her face, she couldn't see a single thing.

Tara and Sophia finally managed to break through the force field and we fled from the cottage. Harvey and I sprinted quickly away from it as we could since we were the ones with the glass ball and the bone. We hadn't noticed that the dove team had caught up with us and were also helping Tara and Sophia to break the force field. Sophia summoned the vines that had enclosed the cottage before but instead of replacing the vines the way they were she made the vines wrap around their ankles and the dove team were pulled into the air and Sophia left them dangling from their ankles while they ran to catch up with us.

Once we were far enough away that we were sure we weren't followed Harvey and I took the items out of our pockets. Luckily the glass ball wasn't cracked and the bone was the same as it was when I first grabbed it. Tara noticed something on the bone that we hadn't spotted at first. There was an inscription burned into it.

You have gotten to the end now it is time to complete your last challenge, break the glass ball with the bone and bring what falls out of it to the wolf that had stood the test of time.

We looked at each other and wondered what or where this wolf was. We noticed that the sun was beginning to rise and we knew we were running out of time. There was a fresh layer of snow all around us since it had snowed all through the night which would mean we would leave tracks wherever we went.

The dove team couldn't be far behind us. "Hey I think I know where we're meant to bring the thing!" Sophia told us quietly as she looked over her shoulder. We urged her to tell us and she started to tell us that while Tara and her were spying on the other team they had passed a statue of a wolf in the forest. We instantly decided to head there. We ran in the snow as if we hadn't just spent the last sixteen hours running around not taking a single break at all. We ran back to the river where we started and then followed Sophia and Tara to where they had saw the statue. When we arrived we saw that the other team had somehow gotten to the statue before us.

Ashley was hiding behind Timothy as we approached. Helena was clutching her arm as if it was injured and she had a couple of scratches on her face and arms. I could feel Harvey tense beside me as he battled with himself to stay where he was or to abandon winning and rush ti her side to see if what was wrong. I looked at the rest of them. Prince Edward had a busted lip and a black eye, Timothy had a bruise forming at his throat and a bruise forming on the side of his face. Ashley looked to be the only one who wasn't injured. She probably made them do all the work.

I made a rash decision, while both teams were busy staring at each other I grabbed the glass ball from Harvey's hands and smashed it with the bone I was still holding. The shattered glass bit into my palm and the wounds started to bleed. A dagger appeared in my hand with a note.

Kill the hare with this and then sacrifice it's body to the wolf

I stared in horror at the note, Harvey actually managed to break eye contact with Helena and looked at what I had in my hand. When he saw the note he turned as pale as I naturally was which for some-one who isn't as white as a ghost normally is a lot. We both looked at each other and then looked at Sophia who was still holding the hare in her arms protectively. We had to do it. We couldn't let them win but at the same time I didn't want to kill the innocent hare. Tara snatched the note from my hand and read it out loud to make sure everyone knew what was about to happen. Sophia looked she was going to cry, Ashley and Helena looked like they were about to be sick, Prince Edward looked sadden by the news and Timothy gave me a hard stare.

"Give us the hare Lady Sophia, he doesn't have to die!" Prince Edward said in a comforting tone while moving towards her with his arms outstretched to take the hare from her and get it away from us. Tara did something I never imagined her doing, she ran up to Prince Edward and jumped on top of him and restrained him. "Kill it Raven, by the will of the gods KIll it!" Tara shouted while she struggled to keep her fiancé restrained. I ran over to Sophia before Timothy could and grabbed the hare by his ears. "I'm so sorry for what I'm about to do!" I told the hare while holding back tears as I didn't want to kill the innocent creature before plunging the dagger into it's skull. Sophia wailed as I pulled the dagger out and the hare went limp. Harvey went over and hugged Sophia. I moved towards the statue while trying to keep myself from getting sick. It didn't help that blood was gushing out of the wound. Timothy, Ashley and Helena backed away from me as if I was some dangerous monster. I carefully laid the hare onto the base of the staue.

Before our eyes the hare's body transform in a flash of light as if magic was leaving it. Once the light had faded all that was left was a plush toy rabbit that had a tear in its forehead. Trumpets sounded all around us as fireworks erupted from behind the statue and exploded in the sky, announcing that the wolf team had won the winter games.

$$20$$

CHAPTER 20

We were brought out of the area the same way we were brought in. Luckily we were given two hours to change for the ceremony so we didn't have to go in the clothes we wore during the Games especially since some places on the clothes got torn. Sophia managed to get her emotions back under control but she was still a bit upset at me even after I told her the hare wasn't actually real. Tara and Prince Edward were off arguing somewhere and Harvey was busy fussing over Helena. Timothy has not come near me at all since the games ended and I didn't care since it looked like the engagement would be over soon anyway. I doubted Timothy would want to stay with me after the reproachfull look he gave me when I first had killed the hare.

I bathed and dressed in a formal long black silk dress that had a lace collar that cover my neck and shoulders. I finally got to put makeup on after having to go without it during the Games, I belive that it had been years since Timothy or any of the others had seen me without makeup. Back in the other world I used to wear the usual exasperated makeup that could be seen on many goths. Unfortunately I couldn't wear my makeup exactly like that in this world so I had to change my makeup style slightly to fight in with the constricting expectations of this world. I did a smokey eyeshadow look with a dark purple blended into the middle of it. I applied a pure black lipstick over my lips and applied a sharp line of eyeliner on my eyelids. I filled in my brows and put a ribbon chocker around my throat while putting silver earings in the cap of crescent moon's into pierced holes in my ear lobes.

Harvey, Tara, Sophia and I were all standing side by side on the stage while the Headmaster gave a speech about what the games were meant to show us. "The games are made to show us our true selves, Lady Darksheild showed us that she is ruthless and determined and she wouldn't let anything stand in her way since she took the initiative that won her team the games!" The headmaster declared as he flipped over the page on his stack of notes om the marble podium.

"Lord Shineblade showed a cunningness and wisdom with how he dealt with the threat of the hag, Lady Rondish showed us that she would do anything for her team to win since she stopped her own fiancé from taking the prized hare from Lady Harnmin!" The headmaster went on. "Finally we come to Lady Harnmin who used her magic to help her team locate the coats that they had to find to complete their first challenge this shows her resourcefulness!".

The audience of our peers clapped for us for a few moments when the headmaster stopped speaking for a moment to allow them to clap without interrupting them. The headmaster's speech was coming to the end so the others and I stood up from our seats as was expected of us. "Now the victors must travel to the ancient temple of the god Oiche, what they may find there we can not say but we pray to the goddess of good health and luck that they return to us after they complete their adventure there!".

We were expected to leave for the temple in a few hours and we had to return two days before the winter ball to have enough time to prepare for it since it wad in our honor. I wore tight dark grey leather trousers and a long sleeve black silk shirt and wrapped my knuckles up in a long strip of black cloth made from cotton. I was tying up the laces on my knee high leather high heeled boots with Timothy finally knocked at my door.

I could tell it was him since he would knock in a specific way. "Come in" I said while focusing on tying my lace. Timothy entered my room and closed the door. He didn't speak so he expected me to start the conversation. "Well out with Timothy! What do you want?" I asked him in a harsh tone while switching to my other boot to tie up the lace on that one. He seemed to chew on his words for a moment as he considered how to say what he wanted to say. "Do you really want to leave me?" He asked while looking downcast.

I finished tying up my lace and then turned to look at him. I sighed before answering, my traitorous heart still love him for some sick unknown reason but I knew I had to make sure this relationship ended on my terms since I couldn't wait for Ashley to finally capture Timothy's heart. I wasn't going to allow him to mistreat me anymore, I was done with that. "It's for the best" I told him gently "We just aren't good together!" I explained sadly. "What do you mean 'we aren't good together' ?" He asked me.I stood up from my bed and went over to the rucksack that Sandra had prepared for me. She mostly filled it with clothes and provisions but I opened up the bag and pulled open the drawer on my dresser and pulled out a few obsidian crystals along with a few small animal skulls and a few black candles.

I stuffed them into the bag, since we know knew that the temple was one of Oiche that fell into disuse after the war of false gods were there was a civil war over what divine people worshiped and since the more "evil" gods followers caused the most destruction and chaos heavy sanctions were placed on those followers so the temple had been left to rot and fall into decay.

"Our relationship isn't healthy Timothy and we both knew it for a long time" I said while slinging the rucksack onto my back "it's better for it to end than for both of us to suffer for the rest of our lives, we won't ever be happy together!". I looked at the clock and decided I would help Sophia pack and try to slip a few more things into her bag since my bag was already full and ready to burst. "Believe me Timothy I not happy about our relationship ending but in time you'll see it's for the best!" I told him gently before kissing him on the cheek one final time before walking out of my room. I chanced a look back and saw Timothy looking heartbroken with tears running down his cheek. I had to look away to prevent myself from being reduced to tears as well.

We sat in the carriage loaned to us as we slowly made our way to the temple. When we passed the temple district the high priest of Oiche had his hand up in signal for us to stop for a moment. "Young worshippers" He greeted us as Harvey and I bowed to him "I heard from my sources that you have been granted permission to enter the ancient temple that was taken from us many years ago!" Harvey and I knodded. "I must ask of you that if you happen to come across some ancient artefacts that you bring them back here so that we may be reunited with them and be able to worship Oiche together with them!".

Harvey and I agreed immediately since we had already decided to bring anything we would find to the high priest first before we could keep it incase it was important to the temple in some way. As the high priest went back up the temple steps and the carriage started moving again Tara asked "Does this mean that if everything we find in the temple has to be shown to that high priest and if he decides that they are all important we don't get to keep any of it?".

Harvey and I confirmed this. Tara sighed but she knew that if the temple belonged to her god that she would also want everything to be brought before her high priest first just to make sure that if anything was of value to the temple that the temple could have it and make use of it. Sophia didn't care either way since even though she was fine with us worshipping a god that was considered to be evil she wasn't going to take anything for herself if it came from a temple dedicated to an evil god.

Just before we left the city the carriage driver told us that he couldn't bring us anything further and that one of us would have to drive the carriage from then on. We debated on who would drive first since obviously we would be taking turns with who was driving. All three of us girls decided that since Harvey was the only man on this little trip that he just be chivalrous and take the first shift. He didn't object much to this but I would say he did it because he didn't trust the rest of us to maneuver our way through the tricky bit of the travel since the first few hours if the travel was the most complicated bit of the journey according to the map.

We were two days into our journey and it was my turn to drive the carriage. The rain was pouring down and I had the hood on my cloak pulled ad low over my fave as I could without affecting my field of vision, we had made good progress we had came to the conclusion that we would arrive at the mountain that the temple was located on within a few hours and I would be glad to be able to walk about for a bit since my lower back was aching from sitting for so long with little breaks in between the long stretchs of travel. The others were either sleeping or reading something since there wasn't much to do in the carriage.

The mountain loomed over us as we approached it. I had tied the horse up at some tree and had unclipped him from the carriage. We started the long hard climb and after a few hours we wished we were still sitting in the carriage from how much the muscles in our legs were cramping.We managed to reach the grand ancient temple of Oiche just before nightfall.It was magnificent, tall pillars of obsidian and I spied some large statues made from amethyst between some of the pillars. The temple was a masterpiece to look at with its intricate design and high towers. Now all we had to do was enter it and look around.

21

— · —

CHAPTER 21

We approached the wide marble doors and threw our weight against them to try to get them to open. When the doors wouldn't budge we had to find another way in. We walked round the perimeter of the temple and looked for a hole or a shattered window for us to enter the temple through. When we couldn't find anything like that we decided to check a bit further around the temple and we discovered this old set of doors that were embedded into the ground and we saw some stone bricks around them with large iron nails securing the doors to the bricks.

Harvey reached down and tried to pull open the doors only to find them locked. Tara already bored and not in a good mood decided just to put her foot through the door, "Well that's one way to do it" I commented quietly while pulling the doors open and seeing stone steps descending into complete darkness. I was the first to walked down into the darkness Harvey followed at my heels.

Sophia had brought a torch with her and she struck the head of it against one of the walls and it ignited in a curious blue and purple flame. She held the torch above her head and the light from the torch illuminated the dark space and allowed Tara and herself to see properly. Harvey and I were happy enough to let them have their light since we didn't want to guide them through the whole temple like we had to do during the games when we were in the forest. Harvey and I searched around what looked to be a cellar to see if we could find a way up to the upper levels of the temple.

While searching through the cellar I had found a box of silver rings on one barrel of wine from what the faded letters on the side of the barrel. The silver rings were made to have an intricate band and the symbol of Oiche in the middle of the ring, set in onyx. The symbol of Oiche is a hawk in the jaw of a wolf. Since Harvey had brought a bag with him to store things in I took the bag from him and carefully placed the box of rings inside it. We searched for a while more and we eventually found a set of stairs that lead upwards into the temple.

Sophia's torch had burned halfway down and soon enough it would go out and leave us all in darkness. Tara had asked Sophia if she had brought another one with her and Sophia informed her that she did and that it was in her bag but they should probably only light it once the torch she had in her hand went out. We climbed the narrow stairs and emerge from the stairway into a hall with high ceilings and massive open spaced pillars. Tara felt out with her magic for candles and when she sensed some she flicked her wrist to lit the wicks.

A few candles in the distance lit up and casted a gentle glow around them but the light looked like the darkness around it was trying to smother it. We all discussed as a group where we should search first. Left or right? We decided to head to the right and then travel down to the left of the hallway.

We walked swiftly down the hallway and passed numerous vacant and empty rooms. Some of the rooms had a few rats congregating in them, we ignored those rooms as we didn't feel like fighting a horde of rats at that moment. We found a grand staircase to the upper levels of the temple and we decided to go up it since we hadn't found much on the first floor. Sophia's torch went out as Harvey and I raced up the stairs as Tara and Sophia scrambled to get the other torch out of Sophia's bag. I darted to the left of the staircase while Harvey sprinted off to the right. "Oi you two quite running away from us!" Sophia shouted at us.

The second floor of the temple was far more promising than the first floor. There was fewer rooms but a lot more stuff in them. I explored a few of the rooms and had a little rummage around in drawers and closets and boxes for things that appeared useful or valuable. Since those who most likely be something of interest to the high priest of Oiche. I found a dagger tucked away in a drawer and it was covered in a thick black cloth.

There was an inscription that I couldn't read on it since I couldn't recognise the language it was written in but I could see that the handle was absolutely beautiful. It had bats carved into it with metal twisted to look like vines going around the handle. I recovered the blade and tucked it into my belt since I didn't have the bag with me to store it in. I ventured into other rooms and found more valuables such as a necklace, a bracelet, a few more silver rings. Once I was certain I had found all that was to be found on the second floor I walked back to the grand staircase and saw that Sophia and Tara were still standing where we had last saw them with their second torch. I sensed movement beside me on the stairs and turned my head sharply just to see Harvey walking down beside me with the bag in his hands.

He handed the bag over to me and I carefully placed the items I had found in the bag. "Looks like you two found quite a few things!" Sophia commented as she looked at the bag that was getting heavier as each new item is placed within it. "And yet we still have a lot more to find!" Harvey sighed as we made our way down the hall were we emerged from the cellar so we could go explore the left hand side of the temple since there was not many ways to go from the right side of the temple to left from as far as we knew about the layout of it.

While travelling down the hall I saw a small portrait hanging on the wall. It was a tall broad shouldered man with long raven black hair, grey illuminance skin, pitch black eyes with just a dot of red in the middle of the eye and the symbol of Oiche is displayed behind him. He wore a long silk black robe with dark grey trim and a wolf with dark grey fur sat by his side. He had one long fingered hand with a silver ring resting atop of the wolf's head. At first I was a bit puzzled at this but then I realised that it had to be the God of darkness in the portrait. I probably should have realised sooner but I had never seen a portrait of him since portraits of evil gods were banned in Highmooreshire around the same time the civil war ended. I tugged on Harvey's shirt to grabbed his attention and I pointed towards the portrait.

Harvey seemed to realise who was on the portrait sooner than I did. We looked at each other and Harvey knodded at me to go take the portrait. I didn't hesitate to run over to the painting and pried it off the wall. The painting was too large to fit into the bag without breaking some of the more fragile things in it so Harvey handed me the bag which was somehow lighter than the painting in a silver frame and he carried the painting. Tara and Sophia were curious about the painting and Sophia had some concerns about bringing an illegal painting back to the capital. We told her it would be fine, we could hide it and discreetly bring it to the high priest when the time was right.

We found another staircase but this time it went straight to the third and final floor of the temple. Harvey and I walked up the stairs this time since we both were weighed down with precious valuables. The third floor was the worshipping area, rows appon rows of pews could be seen. In the middle of the third floor was a enormous. In the middle of the altar was a large amethyst. Harvey scooped it up and handed it over to Tara to carry since if it was placed in the bag it would surely break a few things.

We searched the place a bit more when I saw a long silver greatsword on the wall. I carefully placed the bag down and got the sword off the wall. The sword seemed to hum with energy and magic and I felt a familiar presence around the sword. I grabbed the sheath for the sword from a table close by and covered the sword with it. I placed it onto my back while casting back through my mind if I remembered any stories that featured a champion of Oiche with a sword such as this since it seemed quite important.

Once we were sure we had gotten everything we could carry we went back the way we came and headed back towards the city.

22

CHAPTER 22

Night had fallen when we got back to the capital, the guards questioned about what we were bringing into to the capital. We had told them about the things in the bag but we hadn't told them about the painting or the sword since we had a feeling that we would be detained if we told them about those two things. We thought that they would search the carriage but luckily they just let us pass. Tara guided the carriage towards the Temple of the God of darkness and the god of war and bloodshed. The high priest of Oiche was waiting for us on the steps of the temple.

Harvey gave me the painting to bring inside away from prying eyes. I covered myself in shadows and sprinted out of the carriage. The high priest could see through my shadows and saw what I was carrying. Harvey followed behind me with the bag of valuables. I also had the sword strapped to my back to show the high priest.

The high priest quickly showed us the way to his office and locked the door behind us. He used magic to close the curtains in the room and casted a sound nullifying spell around us so no one could listen to what we were saying. "Quickly child show me the things you have brought!" The high priest ordered me hastily. I first handed over the painting to the high priest. He looked at it in awe. "After so many years we finally have an image of the god of darkness in our temple.

The high priest quickly rushed over to the carpet he had in the room and threw it away from a spot on the floor. A safe had been built into the ground. The high priest put in the code and carefully placed the portrait inside until he could figure out where would be a safe place to hang the painting. Next I took the sword off my back and handed it over to the high priest. When he unsheathed the blade he stood in shock for a moment.

He took the hood down just so he could look at it better. The high priest was extremely handsome with his long light brown hair tied back into a low ponytail. He had a strong jaw and a sharp chin. His eyes were a cool silver grey with a light ring of emerald grey towards the pupil. It is know that when someone joins a temple as a priest\priestess that their eye colour will change to show which god they have sworn to devote their life to. The only hint of what their eyes were before is the small ring around the pupil.

"By the divine" He gasped softly as he read the inscription on the blade.

By the grace of the gods this blade shall smite those who oppose the god of darkness.

"This blade, gods, we presumed it had been lost during the purging of the temples but it's been there all this time!" The high priest explained softly ad he ran his hand down the blade in wonder. Harvey and I stood in silence as we waited for the high priest to explain more. "I can't believe it" He exclaimed delightedly "The sword that the god of darkness himself used in the battle of darkness and light!".

Harvey and I were both shocked by this revelation. I knew the magic I felt on the blade was familiar to me and I guess that the blade had been blessed by Oiche but I didn't think that the blade had once been used by Oiche himself. "Hold on" Harvey asked "How could the god of darkness use that sword? Would it not have to be bigger?". The high priest smiled at us "The sword was bigger when it was used in the battle but Oiche then shrank the blade so it could be used by his champions in future battles!" The high priest explained quickly. The high priest placed the sheath back on the blade almost lovingly and then took the bag from Harvey.

The high priest examined each time carefully to make sure the item was what it appeared to be. The dagger I had found was the dagger that had once belonged to St. Marna, a saint who is believed to have slain the ancient King of the Rat Men when she fooled him into stepping into some shadows and then made those shadows rip him to pieces. She is considered a saint because she was one of the first to have used divine powers such as shadow wielding which didn't really exist until then and only became more wide known when more and more people began worshipping the god of darkness and once they recieved his blessing they too could wield shadows. That is why Harvey and I can see in the dark and bend shadows to our will since we went through the induction ceremony to become apart of the congregation of the temple of Oiche.

The amethyst Harvey had picked up was an important jewel. It is said that each god had to give up one thing when the war of the gods themselves over domains was over. Oiche gave up one of his kidneys and it turned into an amethyst which is now sitting on the high priest's desk. Once the high priest had examined everything thoroughly he had determined that most of the things would be kept by the temple but for a reward he gave Harvey the dagger of St. Marna and he was about to hand over the box of rings I had first picked up when suddenly the sword on the table began to glow and shudder. The high priest picked the sword up and took it out of it's sheath.

A look of procession overtook his features and his mind seemed to be miles away from his body. When he snapped out of his trace he seemed to be in shock for a moment before he declared. "Lady Darksheild it is an honor for me to present to you the Blade of Darkness" I was about to ask why when the high priest spoke again. "For Oiche has spoken to me and has told me that he had picked you as his new champion, serve him well young champion!"

Nobody spoke on the way back fo the academy, Harvey had the daggar strapped to his leg and I had the sword strapped securely onto my back since now I was apparently a champion of Oiche. I didn't really know what my new role entailed but the high priest told me to wait for Oiche to contact me so until then I should go about my life as normal. When we stepped out of the carriage we all saw our parents standing on the steps waiting to welcome us back and to give their congratulations for us winning. Well my parents were probably waiting till the others were out of earshot to tear me a new one.

23

— ◆ —

CHAPTER 23

My father led me to the family carriage and I saw that most of my things had already been packed and put into it. It seems that it was time to head home until after the winter ball where I would then return to the academy and prepare for the final exams. I sat in the carriage and listened quietly to the lecture my parents were giving me. I couldn't be bothered to actually pay attention to word they said so I just looked out the window for awhile.

My mother ordered me to bathe and change into something decent since Timothy and his family would be arriving in an hour's time. I bathe quickly as my maids packed away my things into the places they had been when I came back home for the summer. I changed into a dark grey silk dress with long sleeves and lace around the neck and cuffs. I was able to wear makeup for the first time in days since I left on the mission.

I applied it as I usually would and before long Sandra was knocking on my bedroom door to notify me that it was time for me to head to the drawing room. I sighed as I got up from my vanity but I knew that sooner or later I would have to go through with this. It was one thing to say that I was ending the engagement but it was another thing entirely to actually do it.

My parents sat on one sofa and Timothy's parents sat on a sofa opposite them. Timothy and I sat in armchairs that faced each other and was at the end of the sofas. "Why are you ending the engagement?" Earl Thomas asked me sternly. I looked down at my hands that were folded neatly on my lap and did my best to sound distraught, they wouldn't believe me otherwise. "I'm ending the engagement because I feel that we are not a good match at all!" I said while trying to bring tears to my eyes "I feel that lately that Timothy's attention had been elsewhere!".

Earl Thomas scoffed "Of course his attention will be on something other than you, he isn't tied down by marriage yet so why should he be primarily focused on you when he still has time to change his mind!". "He shouldn't be looking at any other woman Bainne he should be focus on his soon to be wife!" My father growled threateningly at Earl Thomas. Earl Thomas raised both his hands in a gesture that was meant to say "my mistake".

After hearing my reasons for wanting to end the engagement they listened to Timothy's reasoning for wanting to continue the engagement. "Because I love her!" He stated simply, I heard my mother and his mother quietly saying "aww!" In a tone which indicated that they thought Timothy's reason was adorable.

This started Earl Thomas questioning me if I didn't love Timothy. "Of course I love him" I informed them all firmly "however just because we both love each other doesn't mean we are right for each other!". My comment lead to three hours of arguing and the argument ended with Timothy's and I's engagement ending and Earl Thomas left my family home with a red cheek from where my father had slapped him across his face when Earl Thomas had put his masculinity into question. I felt like a weight had been lifted from my chest. I managed to avoid what happened to the original Raven but just because I avoided that didn't mean I was safe. There was still the subject of Harvey and Tara that needed to be solved before I could truly feel safe.

My mother had ordered a seamstress to come to the family home to have my dress made for the winter ball. I took the opportunity when my mother left to tell the seamstress the gown had to be black and dark grey and to not listen to a word my mother would say about how the dress had to be a nice pink. Even after all these years my mother still thinks I'm going through a phase. I also told the seamstress to make sure it was a figure hugging gown and if she could add a few bats to the wrists of the long sleeve gown as well.

The seamstress drew me a sketch of what my gown would look like, and I loved it. The gown would be fitted to cling to my waist and there would be a deep v-neck and the sleeves would be adorned with little bays and lines of silver going up it. The bottom of the gown would flow out a bit from the torso but not too much so it could still have the ballgown look but be very form fitting as well.

My dress was made a few days later and my mother wasn't happy at all with what she saw when the seamstress presented it too us. I was absolutely delighted with it, the seamstress had also added little gems that covered the chest area of the gown which against the black dress made them look like little stars. I instantly thought to a pair of silver star earrings I had in my jewellery box which would go so well with the dress. However I had to calm my mother down before she could try to take the seamstress' head off for doing what I wanted and not what she wanted.

Luckily my mother couldn't really pull the excuse that my dress wouldn't match her or my father's outfit. My father had surprisingly also chosen to have a suit made in a similar style to mine however his didn't include bats but he had a wolf embroidered onto each coff of his suit. My mother went for a white gown with blue gems since it was a winter ball. "Honestly I don't know how I put up with you two!" My mother sighed exasperatedly, although my father and I don't see eye to eye on many topics when we did find something to agree on we became inseparable and insufferable.

The person who would normally had to deal with our antics would be my poor mother. "It's not our fault darling we just look absolutely exquisite in black!" My father told my mother while kissing her on the cheek. "By the way darling you look ravishing in white!" My father winked seductively at my mother. I rolled my eyes, honestly if the ball wasn't in my honor we wouldn't be leaving this early since knowing my parents they would be too busy flirting with each other to actually get ready to leave on time.

Once we were all in the carriage my father spoke to me. "Just so you know my little Raven, your mother and I are very proud of you!". "Thank you that means a lot" I said in reply, I knew that my father had more to say than that. "Just so you're aware we will be trying to find you a new husband tonight so if we call you over we expect you to be on your best behaviour!" He told me sternly. I knew it, my father couldn't just say he was proud of me without there being something else he was after.

I also knew that my parents wouldn't want to waste anytime in finding my a new husband since if a daughter was still into her twenties then according to this world's standards she was not desirable and therefore would be a spinster by twenty five. Little did my parents know that I would also be on the hunt for potential suitors and I already had one in mind.

24

CHAPTER 24

We arrived at the Royal Palace which was decorated with winter themed decorations and looked like a fabulous winter wonder land. We entered the grand hall and saw hundreds of people crowding around a few certain areas of the hall. Many were dancing around the dance floor, swaying to the music by the band. Others were congregating around the food tables. There was a few people around the royal family.

I could see Prince Edward with his striking pale blonde hair standing beside Tara with her deep red hair. Prince Edward was like a carbon copy of his father King Brandon who also had pale blonde hair with bright blue eyes and slightly tanned skin. Queen Elina had light brown hair and dark skin and dark brown eyes.

They were both stunningly beautiful. They were all wearing winter colours except for the King who was wearing his black military uniform and I spotted someone else standing beside the king who also was wearing a black military uniform and looked a lot like the king but still had some of the queen's features. While the King's face was more soft the queen's was sharper. I presumed this man was Prince Sebastian. His hair was shorter than Prince Edward's and it was slicked back while Prince Edward's lay around his face which gave him a cute boyish look.

I spotted the rest of my friends standing in the corner and I went over to them. Sophia gave me a warm smile and I smiled back. She wore a light grey dress that had snowflakes embroidered on it. Harvey was with the girls too but I didn't see Helena. I looked around quickly for her and spotted her talking to Ashley. I looked back to Harvey and he was watching them and he had this forlorn look on his face.

I felt sorry for him, here I was haply being free from Timothy while Harvey was having his heart slowly ripped out of his chest due to Helena pulling away from him. I went over to the refreshment table and grabbed two glasses of wine and I handed one to Harvey. He took the glass without looking at me, he just continued to stare as Ashley whispered something into Helena's ear that made her gasp in horror and looked over quickly at us. My blood began to boil, how dare Ashley try to break Helena and Harvey's engagement! I wanted nothing more than to go over there and slap Ashley across the face and I was planning just that when someone blocked my path.

Prince Sebastian was a good bit taller than me, I had to slightly tilt my head up to actually look him in the eye. "You must me Lady Raven Darksheild!" He assumed correctly as he took a careful sip of his wine that he held in one hand. His suit did very little to hide the outline of muscles underneath it. Since he was fighting in the war it was expected that he would be physically fit ad the soldiers and officers in the Highmooreshire Army trained a lot to keep in good shape. His eyes looked me up and down in a calculated way.

I curtsied and bowed my head in respect "Your royal highness!" I greeted him politely. "I have heard a great deal about you Lady

Raven!" Prince Sebastian informed me as he studied me some more "my brother has a lot to say about the best friend of his fiancé". "All good thing I would hope!" I replied with an easy smile, this was my chance to leave a good impression on the Prince. "Mostly yes but of course there have been a few 'incidents' I hear" Prince Sebastian smirked playfully. I gave him my most seductive smile "Oh and what would those incidents be?" I asked him in a clearly fake innocent tone. He chuckled in a way that was very pleasing to listen to.

"Oh just that you and your friends love to get up to a bit of mischief every now and again" He whispered softly into my ear. I ended up talking with Prince Sebastian for fifteen minutes before one of the King's advisors came looking for him and told him the king wanted to speak with him for a moment, Prince Sebastian excused himself from the conversation and left to go find his father. I wasn't left alone for long since it seems my mother had been watching my interaction with Prince Sebastian this whole time but she was very haply with what she saw. She was certain that if I was able to keep it up then Prince Sebastian would be asking for my hand in no time at all.

Sadly I didn't get to talk to Prince Sebastian for the rest of the night. I got stuck with restraining Harvey duty since he wanted to murder Ashley right then and there. I also had to endure watching Timothy and Ashley making out not even five feet from us while I tried to hold Harvey back while telling all the reasons he shouldn't murder Ashley at that moment, the main reason being that Helena would never forgive him if she saw that. Harvey, Sophia and I were called over to stand beside the royal family since the ball was in our honor.

I managed to sneak a smile at Tara who flashed a smile back at me while giving me a secret thumbs up to ensure me she was alright where she was and she didn't need me to sneak her away from Prince Edward. Out of the corner of my eye I could see Ashley and Sir Darren making out in the corner and I couldn't see Timothy anywhere either. The King started his speak off with thanking everyone for coming then he mentioned the winners of the winter games,us, and finally he went into a very long speech about how he was happy that Prince Sebastian was back from war even if it was only for a short time but he also declared that from the information that had just been brought to light that he was certain that the war would end before spring turned to summer.

Prince Sebastian and I kept exchanging quick glances at one another and just before King Brandon finished his speech to his adoring crowd of subjects Prince Sebastian gave me a quick wink and I had to look away quickly while silently thanking my makeup for hiding most of the blush that must be creeping into my face from embarrassment from Prince Sebastian winking at me in full view of the public. I could see my mother looking very proud and whispering something into my father's ear and his eyes lit up like someone just told him brilliant news. My father's idea of brilliant news is when it involving moving up the social hierarchy and it would bring him more power than he already had.

I danced for a bit. Allowing men who approached me at random to take my hand and lead me into a dance. Prince Sebastian didn't ask me to dance with him but once the speeches ended I heard some people say an army officer came rushing into the hall and whispered something frantically to the Prince and then they both ran out. I presumed that this meant he was called back to war and I wouldn't see him again till after the war had ended but I would need all the time I could get to help my friends with their relationships and figure out a plan to stop Ashley from ruining our lives and I believe tonight she had just shown me a way of how to do it.

25

— ◦ —

CHAPTER 25

Once the ball had ended my parents were very happy with me, they told me I couldn't do any better than a prince! However, even though in my parents eyes they believed I succeed in catching the eye of the Prince they still wouldn't allow me to plan my own birthday party. Like come on you only turn eighteen once, well in my case twice since you know reincarnation and all that, but that wasn't the point. I should be allowed to decide who gets invited or doesn't and what the colour scheme shall be. However it isn't worth the argument that would happen with my mother so I haven't pushed the issue, I just have to hope she doesn't organise something ridiculous.

My mother had even went as far as order a dress to be made without even consulting me about the dress at all. I didn't know anything about the dress until the day of my party when it arrived. She bought me a short sleeved high neck golden dress with a blush coloured tull skirt. When I saw the dress I looked from it to my mother and them back at the dress. I was horrified by it. That dress had more colour in it than I had worn in years. I stood with my mouth agape as my mother stood proudly in front of the dress. "Isn't it pretty sweetheart!" My mother said as she dragged me to stand in front of the dress.

"It's different!" I stated unhappily as I eyed the dress disapprovingly. My mother laughed as she ordered the maids to help me into the dress. To be fair the dress did look stunning however it didn't look too good on me. Gold and warm colours didn't suit my skin tone at all and made me look so washed out. My mother thought I had never looked better and said I should incorporate more colour into my wardrobe.

My makeup matched my dress and I did not like how I looked at all but I had to suck it up since it was my parents paying for the party so the least I could do was pretend to be happy with it since it was only for one day. Tara and Sophia were absolutely shocked when they arrived a few hours early so we could spend more time together before the other guests arrived. Harvey didn't recognise me at first and it took him ten minutes to stop staring at me in shock. I had to explain to them that the dress and the makeup were my mother's doing and they looked relieved, they thought I was going through some sort of mental health issue with the drastic change in my aesthetic.

The colour scheme for the party was the exact same for the dress. I was seriously contemplating never speaking to my mother again for all this but that would be petty and I was still financially dependent on my parents so I had to be civil enough until I had enough money of my own and my own career. For some reason Timothy was invited along with Ashley. I would have to interagate my mother for the reason they were invited but for now I would have to content myself with ruining their night. And I just knew exactly how to do that.

Prince Edward land Sir Darren was also present which was good since I needed Sir Darren here to really add to the drama that was about to start. When Ashley left Timothy's side for a bit I quietly walked up to him and stood beside him. "Are you having fun?" I asked him with a fake smile. Timothy nearly jumped out of his skin since he had not realised I was there. "You look pretty Raven, for once, why didn't you dress like this when we were engaged?" He scoffed.

I shrugged nonchalantly while reaching to pick up a cookie on the table in front of us. "I didn't know that you were open to the idea of open relationships" I commented innocently while fluttering my eyelashes in a way to indicate that my tone was false. Timothy's face instantly darkened "I am not" He seethed while grabbing my arm tightly "where on earth did you get that idea?" He demanded to know while increasing the pressure on my arm.

"I just thought that since Miss Howl and Sir Darren were kissing so passionately in front of the entire Highmooreshire court at the winter ball and since you and Miss Howl are to be wed in the autumn that your relationship was the non inclusive kind!" I told him with a wicked grin on my face. Timothy's face turned so very pale and he looked like he was about to pass out. "You lie!" He accused. I shook my head and laugh at him, "Ask around!" I whispered in his ear "everyone saw it, everyone knows that Miss Howl is not just interested in you alone!".

"Why would you of all people tell me this!" He asked me so quietly it was like a squeak that a mouse would make before it wad flattened by a pile of bricks. I shrugged while removing his hand from my arm, the entire area of where he held my arm was red, "Maybe I like you just enough to tell you about sometime which will put you and your family's reputation to shatters when it finally becomes a very big scandal!" I laughed as I walked away with the cookie I took from the table in one hand and a glass of wine in the other.

I enlisted Tara and Harvey's help in putting together my next scheme. I had Tara convince Sir Darren to investigate something concerning in the garden while I had Harvey warning Timothy that Sir Darren and Ashley were in the garden alone together. I had to convince Ashley to go to the garden. I was determined to have a very big scandal appear at my birthday party, it was basically free entertainment and revenge all I one.

Ashley was talking to Helena and one of our classmates, Lord Richard I believe his name was. "Excuse me Lady Helena and Lord Richard Barracks but would you mind if I bring Miss Howl away for a few moments, I need to talk to her about something!". "Whatever you have to say to me Lady Raven you can say in front of them!" Ashley said coldly to me, I had expected for her to not to be left alone with me away from her friends.

"Very well" I smiled maliciously "I thought that you would like to know that everyone saw you cheating with Lord Timothy and since I told him about it he and Sir Darren are now dueling in the garden!". Helena's mouth dropped open in shock and she looked at Ashley for an answer, Helena despises those who are unfaithful to their significant other. She looked very disgusted with Ashley. Lord Richard also looked shocked but oddly excited, I guess he would be looking forward to watching to men fighting over a woman.

Ashley looked horrified and embarrassed. "Why would you tell him?" She squealed while clutching her hair. "Because I hate you" I declared nonchalantly "and even though Timothy and I are no longer together and I have no feelings for him anymore I do not forgive the way you acted around him when he was engaged to me!".

"So because you're jealous of me being with my Timmy bear you told him about that mistake and now he could die!" She cried.

I sighed with a hint of annoyance. "I am not jealous" I clarified sternly "I would never want to be with him ever again since he is abusive, emotionally and physically, did you know he has hit me a couple of times?". Helena looked horrible at the fact that Timothy had laid his hands on me. Ashley was beginning to stammer about how she didn't know and how he wasn't like that with her. I scoffed at her "I would go save you foolish fiancé before Sir Darren takes his head off from his shoulders!" And with the last word I walked away and smiled to myself at what a show we were just about to see as I heard Ashley running off towards the gardens.

26

CHAPTER 26

Turns out Timothy had asked around and even asked Harvey if it was true that Ashley was cheating on him. This lead to Timothy storming off towards the garden to confront Sir Darren. It seems that Timothy was still a hot head and challenged Sor Darren to a duel on the spot. So when Ashley ran outside to stop them there really was a duel going on and people were already gathering to watch, I was amount them.

Harvey joined me on my right and Sophia joined me on my left. I was excited for the duel, knowing that Timothy would be the one losing. Honesty how could he think he would win against Sir Darren who had been training to protect the royal family from harm since he was five years old. I could see my maids Sandra and Sarah also standing on the sidelines, not sure what to so about the situation in front of them at all. "You adulterer!" Timothy accused Sir Darren "You kiss my fiancé!".

Sir Darren bashed his sword against Lord Timothy's "I swear on my honor I did not know she was promised to you!" Sir Darren said to Lord Timothy to try to diffuse the situation.

Lord Timothy swung for Sir Darren's head but Sir Darren blocked the strike and struck Lord Timothy in the knee with his heeled boot.

"You're no better than that harlot you took to your bed who then went straight into the bed of the man beside you!" Lord Timothy hissed at Sir Darren. This angered him so much that Sir Darren forgot he was trying to stop the duel from getting any worse and he swung his own sword at Lord Timothy's neck.

Lord Timothy wasn't able to block the strike in time. Sir Darren's sword took Lord Timothy's head clean off. As Lord Timothy's head fell to the ground and rolled over to Prince Edward's feet, Ashely started wailing in anguish and screaming at Sor Darren how he could do such a monstrous thing. I had to stop myself from applauding, I wasn't one bit sorry that Lord Timothy was dead, that man had done too much to me over the years and I was glad that he was dead. Prince Edward called for the other guards that he had brought with him and ordered them to arrest Sir Darren for murder.

Dueling was only legal when the duelers has acquired the correct permission from a magistrate. What Sir Darren had just done was murder and he was surrounded by witnesses, there was no way he could talk himself out of the death sentence he would recieve for killing a noble, especially one who hadn't even reached adulthood yet. Sir Darren didn't even try to fight his fate, he accepted it quietly as the guards took him away, tears ran down his face and his head hung low, never to rise from his shame and regret again.

The nights dramatics weren't over yet, Lady Helena started screaming at Harvey and broke off their engagement right then and there. The reason was that Harvey couldn't help himself from making a comment go a grieving Ashley about how it was her fault that Lord Timothy was dead and if she had just kept to her peasant life and knew her place then none of this would have happened.

Even though Lady Helena was angry at Ashley for cheating on Lord Timothy she was outrage that Harvey would ever say something that atrocious to someone when they are at their lowest point. Harvey begged Lady Helena for forgiveness, she wouldn't forgive him and she walked out of my party as a single woman. I comforted Harvey and the night ended without any further incident.

Timothy's funeral was held a few days later and I went to pay my respects to him, well more to give my condolence to his grieving parents and to give the appearance that although my relationship with him had ended I held no hard feelings towards him. Ashley was forbidden from attending the funeral by Lady Helga, Lord Timothy's mother, she blamed Ashley for her son's untimely death.

I was more than happy to support her in her decision and was beside her to provide moral support during the entire service. Lady Helga wasn't a bad person, I liked her as she was also so kind and loving towards me, I wondered briefly how Lord Timothy turned out the way he was when he had her for a mother. I then reminded myself that his father was not much better than Lord Timothy was. "Oh Raven how could such a thing happen to my poor sweet boy" Lady Helga cried into her handkerchief.

I patted her consoling on the back "Oh how heartbroken I was when you and Timothy broke off your engaged but I see now why you did" She sniffed while looking at me with tears falling down her face "that temptress he was with had taken his love for you from him and if only she never gotten involved them Timothy would still be with us" she nearly started bawling her eyes out again "and you and him would still be together!" And with those final words she started crying again. I knew that Lady Helga saw me like a daughter and she was distraught when Timothy and I had broke up.

I guess she held onto the hope that Timothy and I would reconcile at some point and we would get married like nothing ever happened. I felt sorry for her, her only child dead and she would never get to have any grandchildren and she was past the stage in her life were she could give birth safely so it seems she would never have another child.

After the funeral I returned to the academy as the winter break was over and we had to attend classes again. Harvey was a mess, he missed Helena terribly and being in the same room as her while she ignored him was not doing him any good at all. Thankfully Tara and Prince Edward still seemed to be on good terms.

The gods knew I couldn't handle two emotionally unstable people right now who wouldn't hesitate to hurt the person who caused them their pain. Harvey blamed Ashley for everything and nothing I could say would change his view on the matter. I had to constantly distract him from his pain and make him focus on something else. Harvey and I travelled to the woods more often, sometimes taking Sophia and Tara with us.

When I couldn't be with Harvey do to me needing to attend a dinner at my parent's home or attending to my duties as the chosen of a god, Oiche still hadn't contacted me yet so I would have to travel to the temple more often during the week to pray and just be more devout than I already was, Sophia and Tara would take it in turns in staying beside Harvey during this troubling time in his life. However most of the responsibility of keeping Harvey away from Ashley and Helena fell on me and due to us spending more and more time together we became closer than I thought we ever would be.

27

CHAPTER 27

Harvey's eighteenth birthday passed a few days ago and he didn't want to do anything for it since he was still sad about Helena. Me and the girls still bought him gifts and we also brought Michelle, Lydia and Nina along with us to celebrate Harvey's birthday.

Since Lydia and I were the ones who were already eighteen in the friend group we went out to the town to but some nice wine and other alcohol, we were determined to make Harvey's birthday a happy one. His parents were too busy to come see him but they sent him a heartfelt card and very thoughtful gifts to him that they knew he would love. Harvey had a great relationship with his parents and they cared for each other deeply, it was nice to see.

After a few drinks each we began to pass around a bottle of rum and playing truth or dare. At the start the dares were pretty tame, some of the dares were lick your elbow or do a handstand. However as the drink kept flowing and our inhibitions got lower and lower the dares got more wilder and the questions for truth got more and more invasive. At one point I got dares to go to the tower in the west wing and sing a piece of opera music of my choice. Due to me drinking strong alcohol for the last four hours I did the dare without hesitation. My singing on that tower wasn't the best, I was slurring my words quite a bit and halfway through the song I forgot the lyrics so I just started saying random words in Italian.

As time went on we drank more and more and drunker and drunker. Towards half past ten at night we were all well and truly drunk. Tara and Nina couldn't barely stand and Michelle and Lydia were passed out on the floor. Harvey and I made sure to roll them onto their sides to make sure that they wouldn't chock on their own vomit in the middle of the night. Prince Edward came to Harvey's bedroom in search of Tara since she had told him she was going to be in Harvey's room celebrating his birthday. He was not pleaded by what he saw.

"My love are you alright?" Prince Edward asked Tara gently but it was clear as day on his face that he was furious, I was too drunk to figure out if he was made at Tara or at the rest of us for letting her get that drunk. Severely drunk me didn't care either way as I was too busy trying to prevent Sophia from vomiting onto the floor. I managed to stumble my way towards the bin beside Harvey's desk and then put it in front of Sophia.

She was starting to wretch slightly and she had turn a bit pale so I was certain sooner or later she would be sick. "Hhhheey iiits Eddy" Tara siad drunkly before shoving her hand in Prince Edward's face. Prince Edward sighed heavily. "Can you please remove your hand from my face!" Prince Edward told Tara in a tired tone. "Aaalright Princey as his rrroyal highesss wishess!" Tara laughed as she removed her hand from his face and she pushed herself off of the edge if the bed she was sitting on and slid down onto the floor.

"Lady Raven would you be so kind as to help me remove Tara from this room?" Prince Edward asked me helplessly as Tara began to roll around the floor while giggling uncontrollably. Normality I wouldn't hesitate to help but drunk me had other ideas. "Maybe" I replied slyly as I sat back in the chair by the fireplace in Harvey's room.

"Lady Raven please I wouldn't normally ask but I don't know how to handle this situation properly!" Prince Edward said imploringly. I sighed and shrugged and slowly got off of the chair. I stumbled by way over to Tara and yank her roughly off the floor. "Dear gods your also drunk, did none of you consider that at least one of you needed to stay sober to make sure the others didn't get into trouble.

Everyone but Lydia and Michelle, as they were still unconscious on the floor, all said a resounding no before bursting into laughter. I could hear Sophia finally being sick in the bin, it seems that the laughter finally upset her stomach enough to get whatever was causing her to retch out of her system. At least we didn't have to worry about her throwing up in her sleep since she pretty much empty all the contents of her stomach into the bin.

Prince Edward looked like he wanted to cry and be sick at the same time, it seems that he wasn't used to this kind of debauchery where people drank to the point of unconsciousness and sickness. I began dragging Tara out the door ad she loudly tried to protest being dragged across the floor. Prince Edward stopped me as he didn't like the idea of his fiancé being dragged around the corridors by her drunk friend.

He lifted Tara off the floor bridle style and said he would bring her to her room so she could get settled. I shrugged at and said alright before running in the direction of Harvey's bed and then jumping on it and landing beside him. Prince Edward shook his head at us and said he would inform Michelle's, Lydia's and Nina's fiancées to come collect them before we would all get into trouble. "Do as you please your highness!" Harvey yawned before plopping his arm onto my head. I gave a disapproving sound but he didn't care at all.

James, Clive and Ash all came to Harvey's bedroom to drag their heavily intoxicated fiancées out of the room. Soon it was just Harvey, Sophia and me left in the room. At some point Harvey finally removed his arm from my face, mainly because I started nipping his arm and his side to try to annoy him enough to move. He got off his bed and drunk me was just about to turn my back to him and go to sleep when he pulled me off his bed.

"Come on we better get Sophia back to her room before morning!" Harvey directed me towards Sophia to lift one of her arms and put it around my shoulder to help support her as he took her other arm and did the same. We managed to not get seen by any of the school staff while walking back to the girls dormitories. However Helena and Ashley were coming out of Lady Stephanie's room just as we were coming down the hall. Helena's eyes glanced at Sophia and I briefly before they fell on Harvey.

His long dark brown hair was up in a messy bun at the base of his neck and his shirt was half open as he had buttoned it down a bit a while ago since he claimed the room was far too warm. It wasn't but people experience things differently when they are drunk. "My my don't you three look sore for sore eyes!" Ashley commented snidely, she was delighted that we didn't look as put together as we usually did. "Oh shut up you old cow" Sophia growled as we moved past them. "At least we don't go around making out with engaged men" I laughed maliciously.

"At least people actually can notice when we aren't ourselves, your lack of style and inconsiderateness of the way your clothes are present make you seem quite scatterbrained at times" Harvey told

Ashley while looking over his shoulder at her before all three of us bursted out laughing. Ashley was a bright red and she was about to cry from embarrassment when Helena came to her defense.

"Now listen here you three that is quite enough she has done nothing to you!" Helena scolded us sternly. Harvey's merry mood shifted dramatically and he stared down at his feet with a dark look in his eyes. I wasn't about to let the girl that broke his heart destroy the work I put into building back up his confidence and self worth these last few weeks after she broke up with him over one comment without even considering why he said what he said.

"Harvey take Sophia back to her room I have a few words to say to these two!" I ordered Harvey as I let go of Sophia's arm and started to walk towards Helana and Ashley. Harvey tried to stop me by telling me it wasn't a good idea but I brushed him off and once again just told him to take Sophia to her room and I would handle these two ladies. He left me with them reluctantly and once he was out of earshot I went off on Helena and Ashley.

Helena tried to speak first but I cut across her fiercely. "Do not dare to chastise me for how I speak to that one as you do not understand the amount of things she had done to me!" Helena blinked for a few seconds and she seemed a bit feared of me in that moment. "And before I tell that one what I really think of her I have something to say to you!". "And what would that be?, Lady Raven" Lady Helena asked as she took a step back from me as if she was trying to gain as much distance from me in cased I attacked her.

"I am severely disappointed in you, instead of cutting off contact with a woman who not only was an affair partner to a man who was engaged to me she also couldn't help herself to cheating on him which lead to his death and the death of the man she cheated with as he was just trying to defend himself, instead of cutting all ties with her you defend the evil and wicked thing, I'm glad you broke off your engagement to Havrey!". Helena asked me why and I smiled darkly while I laughed at her "because he can do so much better than you!" I savagely before turning my attention to Ashley who seemed shocked at everything I just said, she tried to denie all the things I said but I wouldn't let her, the things I would say to her were a long time coming and it seems that alcohol finally allowed me to say everything as I no longer care about what would happen to me in that moment.

"You are a despicable woman and probably insane too as you don't seem to realise or admit what you did was wrong, I don't know how you justify it in your head and I don't want to know as you sicken me, you think I'm the bad guy here well let me tell you something, I haven't killed anyone bit you have two deaths on your hands. I hoped your fun was worth it because two men are now dead and those who knew them better in life than you ever could mourn their death while hear you are going about your day as if something has happened!". "Listen here Raven but."

I cut a cross Ashely sharply "It's Lady Raven to you and I have one last thing to say to you!" I said as I towered over Ashley and did my best to appear threatening and intimidating while being as drunk as I was, it was easy though since tbe death glare inherited from my father could make anyone cower in fear under my ferocious glare. "If you try to take Prince Edward from Lady Tara I will not hesitate to make your life a living hell! Do you understand me!" I threatened her. She knodded weakly and I walked away to go search for where Harvey and Sophia had gone off to.

Harvey was walking a little unsteadily out of Sophia's room as I walking around the corner. "Did you manage alright on your own?" I asked him while I leaned against the nearby wall since I was still a bit unsteady on my feet, it seemed that by not drinking alcohol for the last twenty minutes had helped us sober up a tiny bit but not much. Harvey closed Sophia door and leaned on the wall beside me.

"Okay how badly did you go off on the two if them?" He sighed as he waited to hear how much damage I caused it the short amount of time he had been away from me. "Well..." I started and I could tell Harvey was preparing himself for the worst "I told Helena that I was disappointed in her for putting aside her morals and defending a cheater and I also told her that you could do a lot better than her!".

Harvey looked at me for a moment and then asked quietly "Did you really mean that?". "Which part?" I asked him to confirm what part I had told him he was referring to. "The part were you told her that I could find someone better than her" He confirmed. "Yeah I did!" I told him as I looked down the hall to see Helena walking towards us. My drunk brain didn't make good decisions and it seemed that neither did Harvey's. "Rave if I asked you to kiss me would you do it?" He whispered to me quickly as he pulled me close to his body. "Yes!" I said without hesitation. "Kiss me" He said and without a second thought I got on the tips of my toes slightly and I kisses him.

I could hear a shocked gasp from behind me but I didn't care. Harvey wrapped his arm around my lower back as his other arm supported my head as he hand buried itself into my hair. My hands grabbed onto his shoulders which I used to keep myself steady. We made out in that hallway for a few minutes and it was a nice kiss, better than any kiss I ever had with Timothy, but that was all there was.

There was no spark or anything that would hint to a possible beginning of a romantic relationship. Harvey was the one to break the kiss and the first thing he did was look at Helena who had been watching us the entire time and the first words out of his mouth were "Don't you have anything better to do than to watch me kiss someone!" He said this in a pointed manner to indicate he wanted her to leave us alone. Helena's mouth opened and closed a few times as she struggled to come up with the words she wanted to say.

During this time I noticed my lipstick had smudged onto Harvey's lips and I tried to wipe it off with my thumb. I didn't mean anything by it I just thought to wipe it off since if anyone saw him with black lipstick around his mouth who knows what people would start gossiping about us. It seems my gesture was far more intimate than I had intended as I slowly rubbed my thumb across Harvey's lower lip. Harvey looked at me with a subtle look that said "what are you doing?" And my action had caused Helena to burst into tears and she ran back down the hall. Harvey let me go as he took a step back from me as I reached into the pocket of my dress for a clean handkerchief "My lipstick is all over your mouth!" I stated as I handed him the handkerchief. He tried wiping it off it seemed to just make the smudge worse. "Stop that's just making it worse!" I told him "You probably need to scrub your lips with a bit of water and soap to get this off".

Harvey knodded as he wiped his lips with the back of his hand, which just spread the black lipstick even more, I made a mental note to stop applying more lipstick than I needed since the lipstick that transfered onto Harvey's lipstick just spreaded more and more each time he tried do wipe it away. Harvey cleared his throat "Well goodnight Raven" He said before walking back towards his room. "Goodnight Harvey" I called to him as he walked away as I started walking towards my own room. I looked over my shoulder and saw Harvey lightly rubbed the bottom of his lip with his thumb in a thoughtful sort of motion that would indicate he was thinking about something. I decided to think too much about it, I couldn't worry about what we just did would mean for our friendship while I dealt with a bad hangover.

28

CHAPTER 28

Harvey and I never spoke about that drunken kiss, we didn't want our friendship to change. The others had found out we had kissed because Helena had ran back to Lady Stephanie's room and told her what just happened. Tara was upset she missed me confronting Ashley as she too also wanted to threaten her.

Sophia wasn't bothered at all from the news, she said she had suspected something like this would happen eventually since Harvey and I gotten closer as friends. Michelle, Lydia and Nina squealed with excitement when they heard and rushed to give their congratulations go Harvey and I when we were sitting on my balcony as if the kiss never happened. I told them quickly that Harvey and I weren't together and that kiss was purely to annoy Helena.

I also made a point to explain this to Sophia and Tara when they came into my room minutes after the three girls came into my room. They all seemed disappointed that Harvey and I weren't together and Harvey was usually quiet during the whole thing. I didn't pry since if I acknowledged it then we would have to have a very uncomfortable conversation about what our relationship was at that point and I wanted to stay far away from that conversation for as long as humanly possible.

Winter had gone and spring had arrived and just as the King promised back at the winter ball the war was over. King Brandon gave a speech from his throne room which announced the end of the war. After a long and very bloody final battle Highmooreshire came out as the victor. This meant that Prince Sebastian would be returning to the castle and take his normal duties over again as the crown prince.

I knew that this would started the next plot point of the novel. I knew that changing the story lines had consequences and some things were just unavoidable. When I wasn't beheaded by Timothy when our engagement ended this meant that the story had to balance itself out. Since I wasn't killed Timothy and Sir Darren were killed off instead to add the drama into the story that the original Lady Raven's death had. It seemed that Lady Helena and Lord Harvey were always destined to break up, there was nothing I could do about that. However it seems that my words had an impact on Helena, she distanced herself from Ashley and for now seems to be sulking with her other friends.

Ashley had begun trying to get closer to Prince Edward. My friends and I all agreed that we couldn't let Ashley take Prince Edward from Tara, at least one of us should still get married by the end of the year which Prince Edward and Tara were meant to since their parents agreed for them to be married by the winter of their eighteenth year.

In-between studying for the upcoming exams and attending a few balls here and there where Prince Sebastian would be in attendance as I tried to get closer to him, my circle of friends made every effort in sabotaging Ashley's efforts in romancing the prince. We would create elaborate schemes to foil Ashley's plans in our spare time and we would dedicated a person for each day of the week to ensure that Prince Edward was not falling in love with Ashley.

With all the drama happening with Ashley I had to make sure to not forget about Prince Sebastian. He was acting just how he was described in the book. He was withdrawn where he would normally be very outgoing and trying to talk to everyone in sight. He seemed he was trying to stay out of large crowds the best he could that wouldn't make him look odd by societal standards. He also seemed weariy of going down dark corridors alone and he seemed to be hypervigalent.

Whenever I saw him I would try to engage him in conversation and did my best to be understanding and patient as he had gone through something quite traumatic just a few weeks ago. It hadn't even been a month since the war ended and people were expecting him to just return back to normal life like nothing had happened which wasn't fair to him at all. From the death toll with the list of names of the soldiers that had died I recognised a few names of my classmates siblings among the dead and I knew that some of these people were in the same year as Prince Edward. Many of them would have been his friends and he lost a lot of them to the war.

I didn't know how to help him through this, I wasn't a therapist 3 there was no books about PTSD in this world as they were as caught up to the modern world in terms of medical knowledge. My main goal was to make sure that Prince Sebastian maintained his position of Crown Prince until the King abdicated and would hand over the crown in early autumn of this year.

On top of everything else going on Oiche finally contacted me, it wad only a brief meeting but he warned me to prepare since something big was going to happen in summer and as his chosen

I would have to deal with it. He also told me I couldn't tell anyone about it and I wasn't about to disobey my god so I kept quiet about what I knew. I practised using the sword and went to the high priest for lessons on how to use it properly since all high priests and priestesses are trained to use weapons that feature the most in the stories of their gods and their chosen.

The royal family was hosting a ball after all the official papers that had been sighed to officially end the war and a treaty between the two kingdoms to ensure that it would not happen again. I was sitting at my desk, studying for exams, since the academy did the final exams earlier than other schools in the kingdom and neighbouring kingdoms, when Sandra knocked on the door. I allowed her in and she handed me an envelope with the royal crest on the wax. I opened it and saw I had received a personal invitation to the ball from Prince Sebastian. The reason was that he considered me a good friend for being there for him since he returned from the war. I didn't really expect this since we hadn't seen each other much but did write each other letters every now and again. Sandra was looking over my shoulder at the letter, she looked delighted. "M'lady this is wonderful, oh your parents will be delighted that the crown prince invited you to this ball as his personal guest!" She told me while she smiled with pride at me. Sandra had been looking after me for my whole life so of course when she saw that I was succeeding in life she was proud of me and herself for raising me to be the person I am.

29

─── ● ───

CHAPTER 29

I looked at myself in the mirror as I swiped one last layer of black lipstick over my bottom lip. I was wearing a sleek black dress with silver jewellery and both were extravagant enough for the ball. I had this feeling that tonight wasn't a night I wanted to be weighed down by a large ball gown. Sandra and Sarah were busy tidying up my room while my mother was lecturing me about how I should behave and what was expected of me.

Sandra had informed my mother about me being the personal guest of Prince Sebastian and she felt the need to come pay me a visit at school and lecture me. I wasn't really listening to what she was saying, I learned how to tune her out ages ago. I was just about to leave when my mother grabbed my arm and told me firmly "And above all else make sure the Prince is actually interested in you before you make your move, do you understand me!". "Yes mother!" I replied as I headed out the door.

The Royal Palace was decorated with ribbons and banners of Highmooreshire's flag colours, green, purple and grey. I saw some of the Highmooreshire flags hanging on the poles, fluttering in the wind. The wolf with a spider in its mouth was the symbol on the flag. Apparently there was a legend around why that symbol was on the flag. According to legend, a wolf and a hunter came across a valley that would be perfect to set up a village, only problem was that there was a large evil spider occupying the valley so the hunter and the wolf thought the spider for the right to the valley.

It was a long and difficult fight and the spider managed to bring the man down and was about to kill him when the wolf jump onto the spider's back and ripped the spider's head off with its teeth. The hunter became the King of the valley which would be later known as Highmooreshire and the wolf lived out the rest of its days happy and well looked after.

I walked into the Palace to see it looked just like it did during other balls except the decorations were different. I looked for Prince Sebastian in the crowd and I saw him standing next to his younger brother and Tara. I walked over to them and I curtised to Prince Sebastian and Prince Edward. Tara looked delighted to see me. "Raven I'm so glad you're here" She whispered to me as we stood beside each other as the two princes talked to a few important officials who had come up to talk to them about one thing or another.

"I'm glad to be here" I told her in reply. Tara and I chatted amongst ourselves for a bit while the two princes were busy doing other things. "Do you think this is how it'll be when you marry Prince Edward?" I asked Tara as I noticed that Prince Edward hadn't talked to her for about an hour now even though he was only three steps away from us. Tara sighed heavily but smiled "I think I'll be sought out more for conversation when I become a princess since I'll be given a responsibility over something that some official or representative will want to talk to me about!". I felt sorry for Tara, I knew she didn't really like attending these balls but I never knew just how lonely it must have been for her to be surround by people but with no one to talk to.

"So what's going on between you and Prince Sebastian?" Tara asked me with a sly smile. I shrugged my shoulders but smile with a bit of embarrassment. "I don't really know what we are to be honest" I revealed quietly since there was people near us that I didn't want hearing our conversation "I know we're friends but at times it seems like we are more than that!". Tara nodded in understanding. "You'll just have to wait until he makes the first move, then you'll know how he feels about you!" Tara advised me wisely. I nodded in agreement.

Tara began telling me about something that happened yesterday when the Palace servants were preparing for the ball when I noticed a candle not far from us was flickering in a strange way, it was as if it was being smothered by something. I focused on it and I noticed a very faint shadowy hand reach out for the flame and extinguish it. The shadow hand grew clearer as the light the candle provided varnished. The shadow hand turned its palm towards me and put its index and middle finger down and then pointed to the gardens with its ring and pinky finger. The thumb was moving in a circle. It was a signal, a signal from the god of darkness himself.

I excused myself from the conversation with Tara and I told her I had to go talk with someone important but I promised I would be back in a few minutes. Tara looked a bit sad that I was leaving her alone even if it was only for a few minutes but she understood that I had to and she told me she would tell Prince Sebastian what I was doing if he asked. I thanked her and I made my way through the crowd quickly and hastily walked into the Palace gardens.

The palace gardens had a maze and I knew I needed to go some-where that was dark enough to be able to communicate with Oiche clearly. I ran into the maze and walked for a dead in that was in complete darkness. It was nearly sundown but this dead end was cloaked in shadow due to a few trees standing nearby. I waited for a moment before dropping to my knees on the wet grass, it had rained earlier in the day, and my head was bowed and I had my hands crossing over my chest. "Hail Oiche, the god of darkness!" I spoke confidently. I didn't have to look up to know that the avatar of Oiche was standing before me. "Arise my champion" Oiche commanded and I immediately got off the ground and to face him.

His pure black eyes with small glowing red pupils bore into me. Oiche looked exactly how the picture we gave to the high priest depicted him to be. He had long black hair and grey skin that glowed slightly. He wore long black silk robes with dark grey trim abound the cuffs and neck of his shirt. His features were sharp and intimidating. I waited for Oiche to speak first since he had ordered me to the royal gardens for a reason.

"My champion I have called you here for a very particular reason" Oiche announced to me "A vile loathsome creature is trying to ruin centuries of my work, I need you to find them and destroy them by any means necessary, do you understand!". "Yes of course!" I said quickly. "The creature's name is Ashley Howl, I want her dead before the week's end... Do Not Disappoint me and remember I'll be watching, I am always watching!" Oiche informed me before he vanished and I had to return to the ball.

I wad intercepted by Prince Sebastian on the way in, I was still reeling from the fact that I actually had to kill Ashley now and I couldn't do anything short of disobeying a direct order from the god I served. I know I joke with my friends about how much easier our lives would be without her but I never wanted to actually kill her.

I felt like I was on autopilot and desperately wanted a distraction so I could escape from my anguinshing thoughts of how I was to kill a young girl even though I didn't like her she didn't deserve to die like Oiche wanted her to which is a very painful and slow death. Prince Sebastian saw the haunted look in my eyes and he asked me if I was alright. I couldn't speak for a moment, what was I meant to say?

I had no idea of what loe I could think of that could trick him into believing everything was alright. When I didn't respond Prince Sebastian gently took hold of my hand and guided me out of the crowded ballroom and he walked towards a rarely used storage closet. It wad dark inside but I could see everything clearly. There was an old mop sitting in a bucket with a few cleaning supplies scattered on various shelves.

Prince Sebastian pulled me inside and closed the door behind us. "Lady Raven did something happen while you where outside?" Prince Sebastian questioned me gently, almost like a lover asking his beloved a question out of concern. "I just... found out I have to do something that I don't really want to do but have no other choice, please don't ask me what it is as I cannot say!" I whispered to him as I looked away from him towards the door he was standing in front of.

Prince Sebastian placed his hands gently on my shoulders in a comforting way. "I will respect your request Lady Raven but know this, if you ever need any help I'll always be willing to help you!" He whispered firmly, his face mere inches from mine. We stay that way for a few seconds, look at each other in the dark, not sure what to do next. Suddenly we both leaned forward, our lips clashed together.

Prince Sebastian's hands grabbed my waist and pulled me against him. My hands reached for his shoulders so I could support myself better as I was standing on the tips of my feet just to be able to reach his mouth. Sensing my struggle, Prince Sebastian removed his hands from my waist and placed them on the back of my legs and he lifted me up and my back slammed into the door of the closet.

We stayed in that closet for a while, kissing each other as we desperately fought to get away from the cruel thoughts that plagued our minds. We found a sense of escape with each other, nothing matter in the outside world as long as we remained in that closet, kissing each other senseless. Our only hope was for no one to discover us in that closet since that would cause a very huge scandal and the consequences would not be favourable to either of us at that moment.

Prince Sebastian had to work through his trauma before he could be in a healthy relationship and I had to focus on killing the heroine of the story, the heroine who was meant to defeat the evil god who planned on releasing his mighty evil horde to aid a wicked king in gaining more territory and awakening an ancient evil dragon that was created personally by the evil god himself, this evil god was Oiche. The god I worshipped and vowed to serve. If I was to survive this change in the story line then I had to adapt quickly since once Ashely Howl is dead the plot to this story will change completely and I would no longer have the upper hand in knowing what will happen next.

30

EPILOGUE

The final exams has arrived and there was an air of anxiety around the academy. People in my year could be seem with textbooks open in their arms as they walk around the school as they try to get just a few more minutes of studying in. Exams weren't the only thing on my mind that week.

I had to kill Ashley Howl before the end of the week or face the wrath of Oiche. I could see Ashley out of the corner of my eye in the exam hall, she looked calm and not worried at all. After hours of exams each day I returned to my room to plot the demise of the heroine. As each day drew to close I became more anxious as I was running out of time quickly.

It was Friday night and we had finished all the exams and the results would be out in a few weeks. Tara had mentioned something about how she heard Ashley Howl was going out on a date tonight with someone and somehow they had convinced Prince Edward to make it a double date so Tara was being dragged along. I asked her where this was, trying my best to appear nonchalant and just trying to make conversation.

Tara told me that they had planned to go to a restaurant a few minutes away from the academy and then they were going for a walk near the woods. The evil dark gods were on my side that night. I was presented with the perfect opportunity to kill Ashley. It wasn't likely that I was going to get a better opportunity than this.

When Tara left to go get ready for her date I took this opportunity to go to the school's althetics shed. I search around in the darkness for a few minutes until I found one of the school's bows. I found some arrows but they were blunt so they wouldn't do much damage at all. I took three arrows and quickly left the shed with the arrows and bow. I managed to get back to my room without being seen and I made sure to look myself in my room as I sharpened the blunt arrows with a small knife I had found in the school's kitchens.

Once I was happy with the sharpness of the arrows I rushed to my wardrobe and picked out tight black trousers and long sleeved shirt. I tugged off my dress and slipped the clothing on. I got the boots I had stored at the bottom of the wardrobe and I pulled them on. I reached for the cloak I had hanging on a hook on the door and I put it on. I pulled the hood over my head and grabbed the arrows and bow. I saw the sword I was given when I became the champion of Oiche out of the corner of my eye. I grabbed the sword and clipped it to my waist, just in case I need it. I climbed out of my bedroom window and scaled down the wall and sprinted off into the night.

I could Prince Edward, Tara, Ashley and some random boy whose name I didn't know. I hide in some bushes outside of the restaurant and I could hear bits and pieces of their conversation through the open window. Ashley was bragging about her accomplishments, she was telling them how she stopped some of the plans of the evil gods. I didn't have to look at Tara to know she was silently fuming. Tara worshipped one of the evil gods that Ashley was trash talking. I waited for a while until they came out of the restaurant. Prince

Edward didn't have his guard with him, this will make what I have to do easier.

I crept along the tree line, making sure I was out of sight and waited for them to stop at any moment. They arrived at a fountain near the trees and this was the perfect time to strike. Ashley and Tara sat on the edge of the fountain as the two boys started arguing about something political. I placed the arrow on the bow correctly and slowly maneuvered the bow into the correct position. I breathed in and released my breath as I let the arrow fly through the air. In a few heart beats I watched as the swift arrow glided through the air and strike Ashley through the middle of her neck at the side.

The arrow went all the way through until the tip of the arrow could be seen poking out of the side of her neck. I watched for a moment as Ashley fell backwards into the fountain and heard Tara give out a blood curdling scream. I didn't stick around for long as I saw Prince Edward quickly looking at the trees where I was hiding to try to see where the attacker was. I turned around quickly and ran off and I didn't stop running until I made it back to my room and made absolutely sure I wasn't followed. It didn't take long for Oiche to appear in my room and congratulate me on killing Ashley.

By morning the whole school heard about Ashley's death and Tara was quite shaken up by the event. I did my best to comfort her but it was hard when shadows would keep whispering things into my ears, they were telling me what Oiche wanted me to do and plan. It seemed that Oiche had a lot more planned for me than I had first thought.

Ten years laterI sat on my cold stone throne beside my husband, King Sebastian. I was wearing a long gown of black silk with expensive silver jewellery. Nobles and officials were in the throne room with us as they tried to plead their cases to us to try to achieve their goals. The sword of Oiche was strapped to my waist and the familiar weight was a comfort to me even after all these years.

I had fought in many battles with this sword and I knew I would fight in many more. I glanced at the maid who was holding my new born son in her arms, little Alex was sleeping soundly. I could see Tara and Edward with their two small daughters in one of the corners of the room chatting with Sophia and her spouse. Sophia met a wonderful man who treated her very well and I was very happy for her. I could see Nina who had divorced her ex husband five years ago with her new wife.

They made a very happy couple. I saw the High Priest of Oiche walking into the throne room. Around three years ago I had finally managed to remove the law that forbade the gods that were considered evil to not be allowed to have their own temples. I also had a new temple constructed in the city in honor of Oiche and his followers who grew in numbers by the day. Sometimes I would think back to how far I had come. I was now a queen with a loving husband and a wonderful son who one day will rule the empire I was creating.

The armies of Highmooreshire had already conquered three of our neighbouring kingdoms and I already had plans in the works to take over three more before Alex turned ten. I could feel Oiche waiting for me in the war room, he had another mission for me after I had to take a bit of a break from doing his bidding since I was pregnant with my son. There was one thing about my life, it was never boring!